UNTIL JAM DO US PART

THE JELLY SHOP MYSTERIES — BOOK 4

DONNA WALO CLANCY

DWC
PUBLISHING

Until Jam Do Us Part
By Donna Walo Clancy

ISBN-13: 978-1720260677

DWC Publishing

Cover Design by Melissa Ringuette
Monark Design Services

Interior Formatting:
Rogena Mitchell-Jones
RMJ Manuscript Service
www.rogenamitchell.com

First Edition

Printed in the USA

DEDICATION

I lost my dad this past October 23, 2017. As the years passed, our time together dwindled. Life has a way of getting in the way when you raise your own family.

One thing that kept a strong bond going between us was my writing. His face would light up when he saw the new cover of my next book or when I placed a new book in his hands for him to read. He called me constantly to see if there was anything new in my writing world that I could share with him. He was so proud of me.

When I was signed by a publisher, I don't know who was more excited—him or me. It makes me sad that he cannot physically hold my new book and read it, but I will hold it up to the heavens, so he can see the cover and I will tell him about it just in case he can hear me.

Soar with the angels, Dad.

Say hi to everyone who has passed before us.

I will always love you.

My heart will hold a special place,

just for the two of us.

I will continue my writing and make you proud.

Until we meet again...

1

"Have you heard the big news?" Janice asked, handing Tabby her double shot caramel iced coffee with extra whipped cream.

Tabitha Moon, known around town as Tabby, was the owner of *Jellies, Jams, and Weddings,* a specialty shop on Main Street in the town of Whipper Will Junction. The shop had been open for less than a year, but was already known near and far for its homemade jams and jellies. Using her Gram's recipes that had been handed down to her and that were already familiar to the townspeople, her shop became an instant success.

After completing her schooling to become a certified wedding planner, Tabby offered that service at her shop as well. There was only one other wedding planner in the area and she was located a half an hour away in the city of Larsen.

"Have you been listening to know-it-all Gladys again?" Tabby inquired, sticking the straw in the hole at the top of her cup.

Gladys Twittle, also referred to as *The Town Mouth,* sat on the first stool at *The Tilted Coffee Cup* every morning. It was her daily goal to be the center of attention by keeping everyone up to date on the local gossip. If something happened in town, Gladys knew about it and if she didn't she would seek out someone who did. She was well known for her brightly dyed hair that always matched the color of the flowers on the dress that she was wearing at that time.

Janice Spenser took off her coat and shoved it under the register counter. She and Tabby had gone to college together. Originally from Carson's Bend she moved into the Starlight Apartments in Whipper Will Junction when Tabby offered her full-time year-round work.

"So, what's the big news?" Tabby inquired, her curiosity getting the better of her.

"Tillie Twittle is getting married!" Janice exclaimed. "Can you believe it?"

"Tillie finally hooked someone? I don't know; I bet it's just more of her mother's wishful thinking," Tabby claimed. "She's been trying to get her daughter married off for years."

"No, I think it's true this time. Guess who the groom to be is?" Janice quizzed.

Tabby looked at her employee blankly. She couldn't even begin to imagine who would marry Tillie who was thirty-six years old, a plain Jane, and a quiet librarian who had no social life. Where would she even meet someone?

"I don't have the faintest clue; who is the groom?" Tabby inquired.

"Cole Brightman. You know, the guy who works at the hardware store," Janice answered.

"Seriously? How would those two even have met?"

"Well, according to Gladys, they met at the *Outdoor Café*. Breakfast is their favorite meal and they kept running into each other at night when they would both order breakfast for supper. They started to sit together and romance blossomed from there," Janice said, relaying every word that Gladys had recited.

"I guess romance can happen anywhere and to anyone," Tabby stated while putting the money in the register. "They say there is a someone out there for everyone."

"Who knows? Maybe they will come to you to be Tillie's wedding planner," Janice snickered.

"Great, just what I need. Gladys is impossible to deal with in everyday life; I can't imagine what she'd be like to deal with as mother of the bride," Tabby replied. "I would be happy to do it for Tillie though."

"Well, at least you know Tillie wouldn't be a Bridezilla; she's too quiet."

"But I'm sure her mother would more than make up for her daughter's calm ways," Tabby said. "Can you unlock the door and man the shop? I'll be upstairs cooking several batches of jelly for that special order that I received yesterday."

"Sounds good to me. March has been a dead month for daily customers. It's a good thing you have all those special orders to keep us going," Janice added. "I guess I'll dust or maybe I'll try my hand at making a bridal bouquet again."

"Do you remember my stalker that used to stand across the street watching the store?" Tabby asked. "It was right before Christmas."

"I remember. Wasn't her name Becky Tillman?"

"Yes, it was. Apparently, she didn't wait until Spring to open her bakery. She opened her new business this past weekend in the empty building next to Greg's flower shop," Tabby announced. "Maybe, she was telling the truth about scoping out my customers for her business."

"I knew that the new bakery opened," Janice frowned.

"I think that I'll give her the benefit of doubt that she was telling the truth and go to her shop tomorrow and check out her wedding cakes. It would be much more convenient to be able to order a cake here locally than to bring one in from Larsen," Tabby said, not noticing Janice's displeasure about Tabby's decision.

"You better be checking out more than her cakes and flavors," Janice warned. "Word around town is that the owner has been bringing Greg and his employees muffins every morning. Gossip at *The Cup* is she's sweet on your boyfriend."

"I trust Greg. I'm sure if she gets too pushy he'll tell her he's taken," Tabby laughed, waving her left ring finger around and strolling to the stairs that led to her apartment upstairs. "Just to be on the safe side, I'll drop a few hints while I am there tomorrow."

Greg Stone owned the local flower shop, *Smells So Fine*. He was well built, extremely handsome, and had jet black hair that made his bluer than blue eyes pop. He and Tabby first met last summer when they stumbled upon a murder together. Greg believed in love at first sight; Tabby didn't. He eventually worked his way into her heart and they have been inseparable ever since. Someday they would get married, but she didn't want to rush into anything and Greg told her he would wait forever if that was what it took to be her husband.

Tabby opened the door to the apartment and was greeted by her two furry roommates, Ghost and Marmalade. Abandoned as kittens in a cardboard box at *The Whipper Will Drive-In,* Tabby adopted them and now they were known as the shop's mascots. Ghost liked Greg better and Marmalade was Tabby's cat. They excelled at getting into mischief together, continually tipping over Tabby's plants no matter where she placed them in the living room.

Shortly after one, Tabby finished up the last batch of jelly she needed to make for that day. She stacked the full jars in the second bedroom which was also used for storage and went downstairs to cover her employee for her lunch hour. Janice was fidgeting with flowers trying to copy a picture of a bridal bouquet in a book in front of her.

"Ready for lunch?" Tabby asked, amused at Janice's frustration at trying to assemble a simple bouquet.

"This is awful," she sighed, holding up the lame looking, lopsided mess.

"We'll practice," Tabby suggested, laughing.

"Go ahead and laugh, but I get the last laugh today," Janice gloated, handing Tabby a slip of paper.

"What's this?"

"A meeting set up for tomorrow at two in the afternoon with Gladys and Tillie Twittle. Tillie wants you to be her wedding planner," Janice chuckled. "Gladys wanted to talk to you immediately, but I told her you were elbow deep in jelly upstairs and couldn't be disturbed."

"I had a hunch that this was going to happen; just not this soon," Tabby stated.

"Good luck with this one; Tillie's got some real crazy ideas for her wedding," Janice informed her boss.

"Great! Aren't you glad that you're my assistant and will have to sit in on this meeting with me and take notes?" Tabby asked, waving the piece of paper in the air.

"Oh, man, I'm going to lunch," Janice said, sulking.

Tabby unhooked the cat door and let Ghost and Marmalade into the shop. The all white cat climbed up into his normal spot on the counter and curled up in a ball next to the register to take a nap. The orange cat followed Tabby into the back room and rolled around on the worktable while her owner put together a gift basket to replace the one that had been sold that morning.

The bell rang on the front door signaling someone had entered the shop. Hoping it was Greg who sometimes visited on his lunch hour, Tabby peeked out from behind the curtain that concealed the work space at the back of the shop. Gladys was marching towards the register. Ghost took off running for the cat door not wanting to be anywhere near the loud woman who was heading his way.

"Tabby, I know you're here; Janice just passed my store on her way to lunch," Gladys stated loudly, scaring Marmalade who ran under the table and behind the boxes of basket filler.

"You don't have to yell, Gladys. I'm right in the same room with you," Tabby said, coming out from the behind the lace curtain.

"I wanted to talk to you without my daughter being around to listen to what I am saying," Gladys started. "Her father and I are paying for the wedding. Personally, I think she's so old she should be paying for it herself, but we paid for her younger sister's so my husband insists that we have to pay for Tillie's wedding, too."

"What are you trying to say, Gladys?"

"She has big dreams for this wedding, Lord knows she's waited long enough for it to happen," Gladys said, rolling her eyes. "I want to set a maximum amount to be spent for this shindig."

"When is the wedding?" Tabby inquired.

"June tenth," Gladys answered.

"June of 2019?"

"Oh, no, not a chance," Gladys insisted. "We are not letting this one get away; June of this year."

"That's only three months from today," Tabby replied. "How many guests will be attending?"

"No more than seventy-five. Donald and I don't want to spend any more than fifteen thousand dollars from start to finish. What do you charge for your commission?" Gladys asked flatly.

My commission is usually twelve percent of the total cost of the wedding and it is added on at the end," Tabby informed her.

"Fine; we called the wedding planner in Larsen and her commission is twenty-five percent so I guess we'll hire you," Gladys sighed. "Tillie wanted you to do her wedding in the first place; we were just trying to find out who was cheaper to hire."

"When you come in tomorrow with Tillie for the meeting I will have contracts for you to sign. We can discuss details then," Tabby said, trying to dismiss the woman.

"Don't you dare tell Tillie I was here," Gladys threatened. "I love her dearly, but this late in life she should be eloping."

Gladys turned on her heels and stalked out the door. Tabby breathed a sigh of relief when the door closed behind her.

"She is unbelievable," Tabby said to the cat as she tried to coax Marmalade out from behind the boxes.

"I'm going to talk to Donald and get his side of this budget fiasco before the meeting tomorrow," Tabby declared, picking up the cat. "I bet he knows nothing about a cap being put on Tillie's wedding."

The bell on the door rang again. Tabby was afraid that the mother of the bride had returned with more secret wedding rules and was hesitant to peek out from the back room.

"Tabs, are you here?" Greg called out.

Tabby walked out from the security of the back room holding Marmalade. Ghost had heard Greg's voice from behind the cat door where he was hiding and ran out to greet his best friend. Tabby put down the cat to reach up and give her fiancé a hug.

"I am so glad that you're not Gladys," Tabby confided.

"I am, too?" Greg asked, raising an eyebrow.

"That awful woman was just here behind Tillie's back putting all kinds of rules in place for her daughter's wedding," Tabby fumed. "As soon as Janice comes back from lunch, I'm going to visit *The Penny Poor Antique Shop* and put Gladys on the spot in front of her husband. I'll bring a couple of wedding contracts with me and pretend I am verifying the amounts given to me to have them ready for the consultation."

"You are one sneaky woman. Gladys is going to be furious with you. You may lose the wedding all together," Greg warned, picking up Ghost who had been patiently waiting for his friend to pay attention to him.

"I don't think so. Donald Twittle has always wanted the best for his kids," Tabby said, confidently.

"I just came to make sure we were still on for supper tonight," Greg replied, putting the cat down and grabbing Tabby around the waist.

"Oh, most definitely! My mouth has been watering all day for shrimp cocktail and fish and chips. Accompanied by couple of beers to wash it down and I figure I'll gain at least four pounds tonight at the fish fry," Tabby answered, brushing a stray wisp of hair from Greg's temple.

"I love a girl who isn't afraid to show her appetite," Greg affirmed. "I'll pick you up at six-thirty out front. It's too cold to walk even if it's only two streets over."

"I'll be ready," Tabby assured him.

He was kissing her as the bell sounded on the door.

"Geez, get a room already, will you?" Janice lectured, getting back from lunch.

"Hello, Janice," Greg said, smiling.

"Hello yourself," she answered throwing her coat in its usual spot under the register. "Don't you have a flower shop to run?"

"Yes, ma'am! I'll see you later," Greg said, squeezing Tabby's hand. "I don't know why she doesn't like me anymore."

"I have no idea," Tabby whispered with a shrug.

"Is he gone?" Janice asked from behind the lace curtain.

"He's gone," Tabby answered. "You have poor Greg convinced that you don't like him."

"I know; it's great, isn't it? Janice said, chuckling.

"You are so bad," Tabby said, shaking her head walking to the back room to grab two blank wedding contracts. "I'll be back in about fifteen minutes. I have some damage control to do for Tillie and her wedding."

"Damage control?" Janice quizzed.

"I'll explain when I get back," Tabby promised.

It was a cold March day as Tabby walked the short walk up Main Street to *The Penny Poor Antique Shop*. She glanced in the window as she walked by the shop making sure that Mr. Twittle was working. He was sitting behind the counter reading the paper. Tabby turned around and entered the shop. Gladys glanced up and a look of panic crossed her face.

"Hello, Tabby. How's the jelly business treating you?" Donald Twittle asked as he closed the newspaper in front of him.

"It's treating me very well, thank you," Tabby confirmed, smiling. "I just had a few quick questions for Tillie's wedding contract I needed to verify before the meeting with her tomorrow."

"What questions would that be?" Donald asked. "I can't believe my Tillie is going to be a bride."

"I'm sure the questions can wait until tomorrow," Gladys interrupted, rushing to the counter.

"It won't take but a couple of minutes, I promise," Tabby assured her smiling and setting the contracts on the counter.

Gladys glared at the wedding planner. She knew that she was there to undermine the meeting they had earlier at the jelly shop. Tabby glared back not letting the older woman get to her. Donald stood there watching the two women trying to figure out what was going on.

"To start I need to verify that my wedding planner fee is twelve percent of the total cost of the wedding and it is added on to the contract total at the end," Tabby stated. "Is that agreeable, Mr. Twittle?"

"Whatever my Tillie wants and she wants you as her wedding planner," Donald agreed.

"Would you please initial here next to the twelve percent figure," Tabby requested, pointing to a spot on the contract.

"Gladys told me that there would be no more than seventy-five guests. Is that correct?" Tabby asked, innocently.

"That seems like a low number to me," Donald pondered, scratching his chin. "I have to admit it's been a while since Donald Jr. got married, but I think there was almost a hundred and fifty people at his wedding."

"Would you like to keep that number open until Tillie and Cole finalize a guest list?" Tabby quizzed.

"That makes sense to me," Donald agreed again.

"Are you done? We have work to do," Gladys insisted, shoving the contracts into Tabby's hand.

"Just one more thing. I need an amount of money that you wish to use as a maximum budget," Tabby said, staring at Gladys.

Donald Twittle now understood what was going on. He figured his wife must have given Tabby an amount that was unreasonable to work with. He'd fix her for being so cheap and sneaky. Sometimes he wondered how he had stayed married to Gladys for all these years.

"This is my Tillie's time to shine. She's waited a long time to find the right guy and I want her to remember her wedding day for the rest of her life. I don't care what it costs just as long as you give my daughter what she wants. She's a sensible girl and won't go crazy. Leave the amount open, Miss Wedding Planner," Donald instructed.

Gladys opened her mouth to protest, but her husband shut her down with just a look. Very rarely did he react against Gladys and her ways; he was usually so passive. But in this case, he was sticking up for his daughter.

"Is there anything else you need?" Donald inquired.

"No, I think that covers everything, thank you. I can't wait to talk to your daughter tomorrow and see what she visualizes for her wedding. I will be in touch," Tabby answered, picking up the contracts off the counter.

Tabby strolled to the front door with Gladys right on her heels.

"I'll deal with you tomorrow," Gladys threatened as she slammed the door at Tabby's back.

Tabby walked through the front door of her own shop wearing a huge smile. She had beat Gladys at her own game again. She would probably pay for it tomorrow at the consultation, but today she would enjoy her and Tillie's victory. Janice noticed her smile instantly.

"What did you do?" she asked, eyeing her boss suspiciously.

Tabby explained to Janice about the visit she had from Gladys while she was at lunch and the secret demands and restrictions that she had placed on her own daughter's wedding. She told her about her visit to Tillie's dad who knew nothing about what his wife was trying to pull in secret.

"Gladys must have been furious with you," Janice laughed, enjoying the story her boss was sharing.

"Oh, she was, believe me. It was weird though. I have never seen Donald Twittle be anything but passive towards his wife, but he gave her a severe look that shut her up instantly. I guess behind closed doors he really does wear the pants in the family," Tabby stated.

"Somehow, I don't think too many locals in this town would believe that," Janice said.

"I wouldn't have if I hadn't seen it for myself," Tabby agreed.

"Do I really have to sit in on the consult tomorrow? Janice whined.

"No, I was only joking," Tabby smiled.

"Thank you, bless you! I've only been in Whipper Will Junction for a year and a half but I already know that I don't want to be anywhere near Gladys if I don't have to be."

"You and me both," Tabby confessed.

"It's almost five o'clock; do you mind if I head home before the snow starts?" Janice asked as she looked out the front window.

"Go, I'll close up," Tabby insisted. "It's not like we're busy or anything."

"See you tomorrow at ten," Janice yelled as she left through the back door.

Tabby started to check things off on the closing list as done. She refilled the holes in the jelly wall from the stock stored out back, watered the plants, and checked the bathroom to see if it needed a touch-up cleaning. A few minutes past five Tabby walked out to the front of her shop to take the open flag down. Loud voices coming from across the street caught her attention. She couldn't make out what they were saying, but they were definitely yelling at each other.

That looks like Cole.

2

The hardware associate was also holding an open flag. He must have gone out to bring it in and whoever he was arguing with him cornered him before he could get back inside. Tabby couldn't see who it was as the person was facing the other way. A large coat hid the body underneath it and all Tabby could make out was the long dark hair that was blowing around in the winter wind. The argument came to an end and the unknown person stormed off up Main Street. Cole watched as the figure disappeared in the swirling snow and then retreated back into the hardware store.

Tabby walked back inside and stood the flag up in the corner so that it would dry overnight. She emptied the register and shooed the cats up the connecting stairs to the apartment. The cat door was locked, and the lights shut off in the shop. The store was alarmed from the top of the stairs.

"Are my babies hungry?" Tabby asked the cats who were following her around and meowing loudly.

She set down plates of fresh wet food and left her fur babies to chow down. The deposit bag with the day's receipts was hidden in the half empty bag of new kitty litter that sat under the bathroom sink. During the winter the deposits were not big enough to warrant a trip to the bank each night; Tabby had to have a hiding place to stash her cash. She figured no one would ever look in an open bag of cat litter if they managed to get past the alarm system and break in.

It would be another hour before Greg picked her up for the fish fry so Tabby grabbed a wine cooler out of the fridge and sat in her recliner to catch the news and the weather. Her eyes kept drifting from the television to the snow falling outside. It was coming down at a steady pace and Tabby wondered why the Brown Bear Lodge hadn't cancelled the fish fry. The weatherman called for ten to twelve inches for the Whipper Will Junction area. That meant Tabby would have to get up earlier than normal to clear the snow from the sidewalk area in front of her shop.

She finished her wine cooler and went to the bedroom to get ready for her supper date. She decided that jeans and an oversized sweater would keep her warm enough during the short ride to the meeting hall. Tabby pulled her furry boots out of the hall closet and slipped them on. When Ghost and Marmalade saw the boots, they wrapped themselves around them thinking they were playing with other cats.

As Tabby stood there letting the cats play a knock sounded at the back door. She picked up a cat in each arm and hurried to see who was knocking. She looked out the peephole of the new door that Greg had insisted be installed so that she would be safer. Her boyfriend was standing there brushing the white fluffy snow off Buchannan. She unlocked the door still holding on to the cats.

"You're early. It's only six o'clock," Tabby said, setting the cats down and reaching up to give Greg a hug. "Hi, Buchannan. What are you doing here?"

"We closed the flower shop early because of the storm. Everyone is staying home where it's safe and warm. Margaret is afraid of driving in the snow, so I followed her home to make sure she got there okay and then we came right back here," Greg explained.

"I don't blame her; I don't like driving in the white stuff either," Tabby stated, patting the dog.

"You mean my brave fiancé is actually afraid of something?" Greg teased.

"I didn't say I was afraid. I just said I didn't like to; there's a difference," Tabby said, poking him in the ribs. "Do I have to prove I'm not afraid by driving your sorry butt to the lodge?"

"No, you don't have to drive anywhere. The fish fry has been cancelled. Ron gave me a call and let me know they cancelled it at three o'clock this afternoon," Greg answered.

"I guess that means we are eating here," Tabby replied, walking towards the refrigerator. "I didn't defrost anything because I thought we were going out. How about a frozen pizza?"

"Sounds good to me. Hello to you too, Ghost," Greg said, picking up the white cat that

was crawling up his leg for attention.

Buchannan walked over to the carpet in the living room and laid down next to the baseboard to warm up. He closed his eyes and settled in for a nap.

"Do you want a wine cooler or a beer?" Tabby asked as she set the oven to four-hundred.

"Beer and pizza; doesn't get any better than that," Greg answered sitting down at the kitchen table. "How did it go with Donald and Gladys today? Are you still the wedding planner for Tillie?"

"I sure am. I saw a miracle today," Tabby laughed. "A real miracle…"

"Right here in Whipper Will Junction? Just what did you witness that constitutes a miracle?" Greg inquired.

"Donald Twittle shut down his wife and silenced her with just a look," Tabby stated. "Apparently, he does have control over his wife more than people believe."

"Seriously? She seems to walk all over him in public," Greg noted.

"He made it quite clear that Tillie would have whatever she wanted for her wedding with no cap on the cost or number of guests," Tabby said, sticking the pizza in the oven. "Gladys was furious. She threatened me on the way out the door."

"It ought to be a real interesting consultation tomorrow," Greg laughed. "I'd love to be a fly on the wall."

"At least I'll have Janice there if I need to send someone for help,"

Tabby laughed, taking a drink of her wine cooler and passing Greg his beer.

"I wonder just how much Tillie will have a say on her own wedding," Greg pondered.

"I'll keep the conversation centered around the bride," Tabby insisted. "Speaking of Tillie, I saw her husband-to-be arguing with someone in front of the hardware store tonight at closing. I couldn't make out what they were saying or who he was fighting with, but it didn't sound pleasant in any way."

"It wasn't Tillie, was it?"

"No, this person had long dark hair and was too short to be Tillie," Tabby answered.

"Maybe it's a long-lost love who found out he was getting married," Greg laughed. "Although it's hard to imagine Cole with a long list of ex-girlfriends. He's so quiet."

"I know. Him and Tillie seem to be made for each other, but you never know," Tabby stated.

The couple ate a quiet supper in front of the television. The snow continued to pile up outside and the wind was picking up. Halfway through the forensic show that they were watching the power went out.

Tabby felt her way to the kitchen to dig out the candles she had below the sink. They finished their pizza by candlelight and decided that Greg would stay the night instead of braving the storm, even though his house was only five minutes away. The power didn't look like it was going to be coming back on any time soon, so they decided to go to bed.

"Looks like we won't know who killed the heiress," Greg said, standing in the doorway of the spare bedroom, waiting for Buchannan to enter the room.

"It was the step-brother," Tabby answered, walking up the hallway to her room.

Not another word was spoken as the two fell asleep listening to the howling winds outside.

3

Greg was up early, even without an alarm clock. There was still no power which meant no coffee and no hot showers. The alarms on Tabby's apartment and shop had battery back-ups. She disarmed them both and her and Greg headed outside with shovels in hand. They cleared off the stairs that led up to Tabby's back door and started to dig out the front of her shop.

The weatherman had missed the mark again as there was over a foot and a half of snow and well over two feet where the snow had drifted because of the winds of the previous evening. Most of the locals were digging out the front of their shops. Working together, Greg and Tabby had the front of *Jellies, Jams, and Weddings* dug out in no time. They decided to go to *The Tilted Cup* and warm up with some coffee and breakfast before they moved on to dig out the flower shop.

The Tilted Coffee Cup was the only place open on Main Street. Two large generators at the rear of the restaurant ran nonstop. The place was packed to the rafters and Wes couldn't make coffee fast enough to keep up with the demand.

Gladys was perched on the first stool as usual, talking people's ears off. Her husband was sitting on a stool down at the other end of the counter as far away from his wife as possible. She stopped talking long enough to glare at Tabby when she entered the door.

The young couple sat down at a two-top that had just become vacant as they walked in. Gladys continued to stare Tabby down from her stool. Wes walked up to the table, flipped over their coffee cups and filled them with steaming hot coffee.

"Now what did you do to Gladys?" Wes asked Tabby, snickering. "If looks could kill the coroner would be picking you up off the floor right now."

"Nothing much. I just helped her realize the error of her ways," Tabby said.

"I don't think I want to know any more than that," Wes replied. "Did you kids want breakfast?"

"We sure do," Greg answered.

"I'll send Pat over when I can; the kitchen is pretty backed up with orders so it may be a while before she gets to you," Wes stated as he walked away to refill other patron's coffee cups.

The electric company repair trucks drove by the coffee shop heading towards the north. Power lines had come down under the weight of the snow just outside of town. The linemen had come in for coffee earlier and informed Wes the power should be back on, at least on Main Street, by noon.

Pat finally arrived at their table to take their breakfast order. She refilled their coffee and went to place their order in the kitchen. Wes returned with their choice of juices and a small tray with a variety of Gram's jellies and jams that came from Tabby's shop.

"Look familiar?" Wes asked, smiling.

"I got dibs on the blueberry," Greg claimed, pulling the tray towards him.

Twenty minutes later they were eating breakfast. Gladys had to drive home her point of how mad she was that Tabby dared to cross her by banging into their table on her way out. She smiled a nasty smile when she saw Tabby's orange juice had spilled into her scrambled eggs and kept walking without so much as an apology.

"I saw what happened," Wes stated as he walked up to the table. "Let me get you a new breakfast."

He walked away with the juice filled plate. Donald Twittle approached the table wearing a frown. He stopped next to Tabby and took out his wallet.

"I want to apologize for my immature wife. Sometimes, I don't know why I stay married to her. I guess love outweighs everything else," he admitted, shaking his head. "Breakfast is on me this morning."

"That's not necessary, Mr. Twittle," Tabby stated.

"Please call me Donald and yes, it is," he insisted. "I should have known she would try to pull something with Tillie's wedding; Gladys is so selfish and she always has been. Thanks to you my daughter will have the wedding she wants and deserves."

"I'm so glad you're not mad at what I did," Tabby replied. "I just felt bad for Tillie."

"You continue to look out for my girl and I'll be eternally grateful," Donald smiled as he walked away.

Pat returned with a plate of fresh food for Tabby. The couple finished eating and got ready to leave. Wes informed them they were good to go as Donald paid their bill before he left. Greg left Pat a good-sized tip and they walked up Main Street to dig out Greg's business. As they approached the front of the flower shop they realized that the snow had already been removed the entire length of the sidewalk and from around his front door.

"Who did this?" Greg wondered, looking around.

Becky Tillman came out of the front door of her new bakery that was in the building next to Greg's.

"You're all set to open as soon as the electricity comes back on," she said, smiling at Greg as she walked up to him. "Oh… hi Tabby."

"Hello, Becky," Tabby said, as she took hold of Greg's hand. "This was awful nice of you to do this for my fiancé."

"Yeah, whatever," Becky grumbled, as she dismissed Tabby's existence. "Are you going to open the flower shop today, Greg?"

"It depends upon when we get the electricity back," Greg answered, wanting to get inside away from the brewing cat fight. "I need to go to check on my flowers. Thanks for shoveling."

"I guess now that you're open, we will have to schedule an appointment for a cake tasting," Tabby commented, as she watched Becky's eyes follow Greg as he went through the door.

"I guess we will."

"Becky, you do realize that Greg is not available?" Tabby questioned, crossing her arms in front of her chest.

"Yeah, but we'll see for just how long," Becky answered, walking away. "Do your best to keep him, girlfriend; do your best."

Tabby flew over to the bakery door and opened it. Standing in the open door, she stared Becky down.

"There will be no cake tasting and there will be no referrals from any of my wedding consultations. Greg is mine and you stay away from him. Do you understand me?" Tabby demanded as she walked up to the counter in the bakery.

"I don't see any ring on his finger and until I do, Greg is fair game. Like I said; do your best because I'm going to do mine to push you right out of the picture," Becky confirmed. "Now, get out of my shop."

"Don't mess with me, Becky. This will be your one and only warning," Tabby cautioned as she stormed out of the bakery, slamming the door behind her.

Tabby blew into the flower shop and plunked herself down in front of the fountain. Greg was in the cooler checking on the condition of the live flowers. She concentrated on slowing down her breathing and calming herself so that her heart would stop beating out of her chest. Tears started forming in her eyes. Her hands were clenched so tight that the knuckles were turning white from the lack of blood flow.

How dare she? Who the heck does she think she is?

Tabby ran her hand through the lily pond water. The lack of electricity, causing the loss of heat in the shop, made the water colder than usual. The unexpected coolness of the water momentarily made her forget the aggravation that she was feeling.

Greg had been watching her from the cooler. As much as he didn't like to see her hurting the way she was, he was glad to know that she loved him enough to be that upset. He could see that he would have to be the one to set Becky straight and send her and her thoughts elsewhere. He walked up behind Tabby and set his hand on her shoulder. She looked up at him with lingering tears and he knelt down next to her.

"You have nothing to worry about you know," Greg whispered.

"What an arrogant little..." Tabby stated, punching the water. "She had the nerve to tell me she was going to push me out of the picture."

"You know that will never happen," Greg insisted. "Don't let her get to you."

"She was just so sure of herself," Tabby muttered.

"Do you trust me?" Greg asked as he took hold of Tabby's hand.

"Of course; it's her that I don't trust. I don't like the fact that she works right next door to you," Tabby lamented. "She told me if you didn't have a ring on your finger, then you were fair game."

"I'm taken; that is all you need to remember," Greg whispered as he gently held up her hand with the diamond ring on it. "You are the future Mrs. Gregory Stone; no one else will ever take that away from you."

Becky was watching through the window. Tabby spotted her, but Greg didn't as his back was to the front of the store. She wrapped her arms around Greg's neck and gave him an extra-long kiss.

"She's looking in the window, isn't she?" Greg asked, when he came up for air.

"Yes, she is," Tabby admitted.

"Your bad, Tabitha Flower Moon; but that's why I love you," he smiled.

Greg stood up and Becky hurried away from the front window not wanting to be seen. Tabby smiled knowing she was secure in her relationship and that her and Greg would be together forever; Becky or no Becky.

4

Tabby returned to her shop and opened the doors. She had called Janice to tell her to stay home and enjoy the snow day. This meant that Tabby would have to face Gladys and Tillie alone with no back-up. The only saving grace was that she didn't think that Gladys would try to pull anything more knowing Tabby would go right to her husband if she did.

It was one forty-five and Tabby had to get ready for the Tillie's consultation. She gathered the contracts that Donald had already signed and the books that showed samples of flowers, cakes, and venues. She would have to go back to using *A Slice of Heaven Bake Shop* in Larsen for Tillie's wedding cake as she decided she would never send any business Becky's way.

Exactly at two o'clock Tillie and Gladys came through the front door; Gladys leading the way and Tillie following with her head down as she walked.

"Tillie, I am so glad to see you," Tabby greeted the bride-to-be with a smile. "Congratulations and I am so happy for you."

"Let's get this meeting started; I have things to do," Gladys snapped.

"Let's get something straight right from the beginning, Gladys. This meeting is for Tillie, not you. If you have things to do, go do them as your husband signed all the contracts already and you don't really even have to be here," Tabby reminded her.

For the first time since she entered the shop, Tillie looked up and smiled at Tabby. You could see the steam coming out of Gladys' ears. She stormed over to the consult table and plopped down in the chair almost tipping it over sideways. Tabby couldn't be sure, but she thought she heard a quiet chuckle come from Tillie's direction.

"Shall we begin," Tabby said to Tillie.

They sat together on the opposite side of the table away from Gladys. Tillie was beaming at the attention she was receiving and that she was out from under her mother's thumb.

"Is June 10 still the date you want?"

"Yes, it is," Tillie answered. "Is that enough time to plan a wedding?"

"Not really," Gladys piped up. "Why don't you just elope?"

"Oh, Mother," Tillie whispered, tearing up.

"That's it, I've already had enough. Gladys, if you can't be supportive and offer positive ideas then you need to leave. I will go and get your husband and tell him how you are ruining this consultation and hurting your daughter," Tabby demanded. "What's it going to be?"

You can't tell me to leave; I have a right to be here. We're paying for this wedding after all," Gladys insisted. "I have full say on what goes on."

"Not according to Tillie's dad. He wants his daughter to have the wedding of her dreams. Are you going to leave on your own or will I go get him?" Tabby said.

"Well, I never...," Gladys mumbled, getting up from the table.

"Tillie will do fine without you here, in fact she'll probably do better," Tabby stated, smiling at Tillie. "Please leave; we have lots of work to do."

"Good bye, Mother," Tillie spoke up. "I'll come to the store when we are done."

The bride's mother stormed out the door not even bothering to put on her coat. She ran full tilt into Jen, Tabby's best friend, who was trying to enter the jelly shop.

"Get out of my way," Gladys yelled, pushing Jen to one side. "You're as bad as she is."

Gladys stormed up the street in a huff. Jen watched her leave noting that her dress looked like a field of tiger lilies swaying in the wind as Gladys waddled her way back to her antique shop.

"What did you do to Hurricane Gladys this time?" Jen asked, not realizing that Tillie was in the store.

"She stood up to my Mother and saved my wedding," Tillie said, coming out of the corner of the consultation area.

"Oh, Tillie, I didn't know you were here," Jen murmured.

"That's okay, Jen. I know what most of town thinks about my mother and unfortunately they are not wrong," Tillie said, hanging her head.

"I'm sorry, Tillie, I really am."

"This is supposed to be a happy occasion," Tabby reminded everyone present. "Did you need something, Jen?"

"I just wanted to make sure you were going to be at the bookstore this Saturday for the book signing," Jen stated. "You promised to bake cookies, remember?"

"I'll be there," Tillie announced, all excited. "I'm bringing every book that I have written by Wayne Ford and having him sign them all. And I'm going to buy his new release, Murder by Murder, and have him sign that one, too."

"You like mysteries, Tillie?" Jen inquired.

"I love mysteries; it's my favorite genre," the bride admitted.

"You should come to our book club. We meet on Tuesday nights at the bookstore where we discuss the book we read over the previous week. We read mostly mysteries; it's fun and I think you'd like it," Jen said.

"It is fun, and the discussions can get pretty lively," Tabby agreed. "I'll be there on Saturday and I'll bring cookies, lots of cookies."

"Good. Then I'll be on my way so you two can get back to what you were doing; planning an awesome wedding," Jen said, heading for the door. "Have fun, Tillie."

They returned to the table and Tabby closed the books that were opened on the table.

"Now that your mother is not here, I want you to tell me what you really want for your dream wedding. The first thing I need to know is do you have a theme picked out?"

"Yes, Cole and I want a breakfast wedding. Does that sound weird?" Tillie inquired.

"Your mother told me you met over breakfast. It doesn't sound weird at all. If it's something that is special to the both of you, let's go with it."

"My mother thought it was foolish," Tillie said, sighing. "Can I tell you something, Tabby?"

"Sure, what is it?"

"I know she tried to sabotage my wedding; my Dad told me. He also told me to have the wedding of my dreams. He inherited money from his parents many years ago, a great sum I might add, and he doesn't care if my mother doesn't want to spend it. I want to have a nice wedding, but not one that will wipe out my dad's inheritance."

"We can do this, Tillie, don't you worry," the wedding planner confirmed. "Do you want a sit-down meal or a buffet?"

"A buffet would be better. We want to be married at eight a.m. on Saturday morning in Cole's backyard and then everyone will follow the path from his back yard to the Brown Bear Lodge for a wedding breakfast. We already reserved the hall."

"That sounds like fun. We'll need to rent chairs for the service," Tabby said, starting a list. "How about flowers? Do you have a favorite?"

"I love red roses. The color will fit in with our theme of strawberries."

"Strawberries?"

"Yes, Cole and I met while we were each trying to take the last of the strawberries on the buffet at *The Outer Café.* We want our menu to feature strawberry recipes."

"We can come up with a menu later. You can't have all strawberry items as some people may not like them."

"Oh, we realize that. We want all kinds of breakfast items on the buffet; waffles, pancakes, muffins, bacon, and more."

"Sounds yummy! What about a wedding cake?"

"Cole and I talked about it. We would like layers of sponge cake with strawberries and whipped cream in between them. Cole called it a free-standing strawberry shortcake."

"I use *A Slice of Heaven Bakery* in Larsen. They are very reputable, and their cakes are to die for," Tabby suggested.

"What about the new bakery here in town?" Tillie asked.

"I haven't had a chance to see or taste their product yet," Tabby stated, keeping the real reason to herself, but not lying to Tillie when giving her an answer.

"Cole and I would like you to make the favors. You know those small jars of jelly you gave out to thank the locals for helping you when your apartment was broken into; we would like those filled with your strawberry jam to give out to our guests. Can that be done?" Tillie inquired.

"Most definitely. Let's work together to figure out what your reception area will look like and what flowers we need to order," Tabby suggested.

Two hours flew by as the wedding planner and her client tossed ideas back and forth until they had a well-formed plan. It was simple, yet unique, and exactly what Tillie wanted for her dream wedding. The bride was bubbling over with excitement.

Tillie was given two assignments. First, her and Cole had to come up with their guest list so that Tabby would have a count for invitations as they needed to go out as soon as possible. Second, she needed to look through bridal magazines for a wedding gown. The ceremony was only three months away and she didn't have that long to find a gown and have it fitted.

The bride gave her wedding planner a huge hug as they stood up. She had tears in her eyes. Tabby realized this was the first time that Tillie had been out from under her mother's thumb and been able to speak for herself. The quiet librarian was a good person once you got to know her. Tabby knew that she had a new friend even after the wedding was over.

"I told my dad you were the best and would be able to envision what I wanted. I don't care what my mother says, this is going to be the best wedding Whipper Will Junction has ever seen. The locals will be talking about it for years. I will get a guest count to you within forty-eight hours. Cole and I will work on the list tonight at supper," Tillie promised.

"I'll call the bakery and order your cake as soon as we know how many guests they'll be; that will determine how many tiers we need. Do you want to get your own cake topper, or shall I order one for you?"

"I know just the one I want. I'll get it to you this weekend," Tillie said.

"Great! We got a lot done today. I'll start working on ordering what we need for the wedding and you get me that guest list as soon as you can," Tabby instructed.

Not one customer had come in while Tabby was working with her bride. Even though the electricity had come back on at three o'clock, the snow storm had pretty much kept everyone at home. She decided that she would close her store early and head up to see how her Greg was doing with his flowers now that the heat was back on in his shop.

Tabby locked the front door and went upstairs to feed Ghost and Marmalade. She had full intentions of asking Greg to have supper at the diner instead of cooking supper herself. She was exhausted mentally and emotionally and didn't feel like cooking.

She strolled up Main Street towards the north end of town. As she passed *The Penny Poor Antique Shop* she could see Tillie excitedly talking to her dad who was closing out the register at the counter. Gladys was listening from the back corner with an obvious frown on her face.

Tabby knew she was going to pay dearly for this last act of defiance against Gladys. The last punishment was a ruined breakfast; what would it be this time she wondered? She reached the front door of the flower shop. The closed sign was still up in the window which meant that Greg never opened. Tabby also noticed that the bakery was closed next door. Maybe Becky had given up and gone home.

The warmth of a turned-up thermostat met Tabby's face as she entered the shop. The fountain water was gurgling with the return of the electricity and Greg was busy sorting dead flowers out of the buckets in the walk-in refrigerator. He spotted her and mouthed he'd be right out. She sat down next to the frog fountain and talked to Horatio, the head frog, while she waited for Greg.

"I need you to watch over your owner while I'm not here," Tabby whispered to the frog. "If that Becky person comes in here, you give her a bad case of warts; a double dose is just fine with me."

"Talking to the frogs again?" Greg asked, smiling.

"They happen to be very good listeners," Tabby said, picking up several dead flowers that Greg had dropped.

"How did your visit go with Tillie and her mother?"

"The meeting went fine once we threw Gladys out," Tabby answered.

"Are you kidding me? Do you have a death wish?"

"No, I don't, but I couldn't take her snide comments about Tillie eloping anymore. She made her daughter cry and I asked her to leave."

"I can't wait to see the backlash on this one," Greg stated, rolling his eyes.

"Whatever; I have Tillie's dad on my side, so I'm really not worried about it."

"I hope you're right. I lost about twenty percent of my live flower stock to the cold temperatures once the power went out; mostly the ones in the main shop space not the refrigerated ones."

"It could have been worse. Do you need help with anything?"

"No, but I did have someone else offer to help me today," Greg said, waiting for a reaction.

"She didn't, seriously? Are you telling me that Becky came in here after I left?" Tabby asked, furious.

"Yes, she did. I tried to tell her that we were engaged, but she didn't want to listen. She kept changing the subject, so I bluntly told her I had no interest in her and she needed to back off."

"What did she do?"

"She calmly walked out the door stating that she would change my mind no matter what I was saying to her now," Greg answered, shrugging his shoulders. "Some people can't take no for an answer, I guess."

"I've told her and now you've told her; what is it going to take to get through to her?" Tabby questioned.

"I don't know, but I'm hungry. Do you want to go to the diner for super?" Greg asked.

"I was going to suggest the same thing. You see, we belong together; great minds think alike," Tabby smiled.

The couple were enjoying a nice quiet dinner in one of the back booths at the diner when the Twittles walked in for super. Tillie spotted Tabby first and waved enthusiastically. The bride-to-be and her parents were seated in a booth on the opposite end of the diner.

"Looks like you have a new friend," Greg said, amused at the greeting that Tabby received from Tillie.

"She's really a nice person," Tabby insisted. "Jen invited her to come to the book club. She got all excited; I don't think she has any social life at all."

"With a mother like she has, it's no wonder that everyone stays away," Greg mumbled.

5

The seasons changed. Summer arrived and the town of Whipper Will Junction came to life with the beginning of a new tourist season. Memorial Day passed with the Summer Kick-Off Weekend and a good time was had by all who celebrated.

The past two months Tabby had worked closely with Tillie to complete all the wedding details and prepare for her upcoming marriage. The big day was only a week away.

The guest list had been finalized and one hundred and sixty people were attending. Most of the locals had been invited as they had watched Tillie grow up and were friends with her parents. Cole didn't have much family to speak of; both of his parents were deceased and he only had one brother who was flying in for the wedding and would be his best man. He had a few friends from work that would also be attending.

Becky Tillman had been her usual obnoxious self all winter, getting under Tabby's skin and still trying to lure Greg out of the relationship that he was in. Tabby stayed far away from Becky in public as every time they were near each other a verbal fight would break out much to the delight of Gladys. The town mouth would broadcast what was said, word for word, from her stool the next morning at the coffee shop.

Then, she was more than happy to give her opinion announcing that Greg would be so much better off with Becky.

Tabby held her head high and tried to ignore Gladys and her rantings; she was used to it. Greg, on the other hand was not used to being included in her daily speeches to the locals. He spoke to Donald Twittle in private and requested that he speak to his wife so she would cease voicing her opinions regarding Greg and Tabby's relationship. It didn't help as Gladys continued blabbing to anyone who would listen.

It was Friday, the day before Tillie's wedding. Tabby spent most of the day at the reception hall making sure everything was perfect for the wedding breakfast. Greg had delivered the centerpieces and dropped of the bouquets and boutonnieres at Cole's house.

The bride stopped at the hall in the late afternoon. She was thrilled with the way it turned out. Round tables that had been covered with red tablecloths and set with white napkins, plates, and silverware surrounded the wooden dance floor. Centerpieces of red roses, fake strawberries, and white baby's breath had been placed on each table.

The head table was centered at the top of the dance floor for the bride and groom and their bridal party of two. Matching champagne flutes and silver jelly trays engraved with the words bride and groom were set at the center seats. A small floral centerpiece containing cascading red roses and fake strawberries stood out against the white table linen in front of where the bride and groom would sit.

Tabby had set a small jar of strawberry jelly at each place setting tied up in a gold silk bag with a red ribbon. A small card had been attached to each one thanking the guest for coming.

A Slice of Heaven from Larsen had delivered the four-tiered strawberry shortcake wedding cake which would be set up on its own table to the right of the dance floor. It was decorated around each tier with red sugar roses and the bride and groom that Tillie chose sat proudly on top. It was being stored in the walk-in until right before the guests arrived because of the whipped cream layers.

A table for wedding gifts and a wishing well that would hold cards had been placed next to the cake table. The buffet tables formed an L-shape at the front of the room opposite the head table.

After Tillie approved everything and left, Tabby made a trip to Cole's house to check on the flowers that had been delivered there. She had been given a key to the house so that she had easy access for anything relating to the wedding.

The bridal bouquet matched the centerpiece on the head table except on a smaller scale. The matron of honor's bouquet was eight red roses and baby's breath tied together with a white satin ribbon. All the men's boutonnieres were red roses. Tillie wanted a corsage for her mother, but Gladys insisted it was a waste of money and informed her daughter she wouldn't wear it.

As Tabby was counting the boutonnieres a loud discussion started upstairs that caught her attention. She moved towards the stairs that led to the second floor to see if she could make out who was arguing and what they were saying.

"I don't care what you say. That marriage is over and was a long time ago," a male voice yelled.

"You never legally got a divorce. Stephanie disappeared and I know you filed papers when she had been gone for three years, but the divorce was never finalized; you are still married."

"Not as far as I am concerned; she's been gone ten years without a word."

"It's up to you, but I think you're going about this the wrong way. Have you told Tillie about Stephanie?"

"No, and I don't plan to. Tillie and I are very happy. Why would I bother her with something from over ten years ago that doesn't even concern her? No, Jerry, you are not going to ruin this for me. If you can't keep your mouth shut then I must insist that you leave now. You came between me and Stephanie and I am not going to let you destroy my life again."

"Stephanie was trailer trash. You deserved better."

"If she was trailer trash, why did you want her for yourself?" Cole demanded. "Maybe you're the one responsible for her disappearance. Did you lose your temper when she rejected you and kill her? Don't think I haven't thought about it over the years, but it was something I could never prove one way or another."

"Why did you ask me here to be your best man if you thought that?"

"Because you're the only family I have left and I don't know what really happened to Stephanie. She could have left of her own accord, but for the life of me I don't know why. Anyway, are you going to agree to keep your mouth shut or are you going to leave right now?"

"You're the groom; we'll do it your way. I still think you are wrong not telling Tillie, but I'll keep my mouth shut and head back home tomorrow. I hope things work out for you this time, big brother; I really do."

Tabby knew the conversation was coming to an end and didn't want to get caught listening in on the brothers. She hurried out the back door with the box that held the bridal bouquet, matron of honor flowers, and Donald's boutonniere as she would have to bring these to the Twittle house in the morning for pictures. She hurried through the back yard towards the Bear's Lodge. What she didn't know was that Jerry had seen her leaving the house through the upstairs window. He wondered just how much of their conversation she had overheard.

She put the flowers in the walk-in, did a last-minute check on the reception hall, and then hurried back to her shop to see how the day had gone for Janice and to verify that Janice would be there the next morning to open the shop.

Tabby knew she was going to have to be at the hall early in the morning to finish last minute details and then go to the Twittle house to help the bride get ready. The photographer would take family pictures at the house and then the limo would take everyone to Cole's house.

At six a.m. Tabby walked through the doors of the reception hall. The place was already bustling. The caterer and his people were filling steam trays and setting wrapped platters of food around the buffet tables. The jelly trays had already been filled and were ready to put out on the guest tables. The wedding planner grabbed the bride and groom's jelly trays and the matching Best Man and Matron of Honor trays to put them on the head table. She checked the flowers for freshness and watched as the wedding cake was being assembled on the cake table.

After making sure the head table and all it contained was perfect she turned around and saw Becky carrying in trays of muffins that she placed on the buffet table. Tabby was enraged that this woman dared to show her face here. She stormed over and confronted Becky demanding to know why she was there.

"For your information, the caterer hired me to do the baking. He knows a great baker when he samples the food, which is more than I can say for you," Becky said, flippantly. "Everyone in town will be at this wedding and they will see just how excellent a baker I am."

"Drop off your food and clear out of here," Tabby demanded. "I'll take this up with the caterer."

"It's too late for you to do anything about it. You don't have time to replace all the food I baked," Becky boasted. "Live with it, loser."

Tabby had all she could do to control herself and she knew her face was turning redder by the minute. She had to walk away and let the caterer take care of it.

"Leave your food in the kitchen," Tabby said, trying to keep her voice in control. "I don't want to see your face out here again, do you understand?"

"You lose again. I am one of the waitresses the caterer hired to serve the buffet," Becky answered, smiling.

"We'll see about that. You'll be out of here in less than one minute," Tabby insisted.

Tabby returned with the caterer in tow. He informed Becky that he could not use her to serve at the wedding reception. She vehemently opposed anything he said to her arguing every step of the way. The caterer told her the wedding planner has the final say and she had to go.

"I'll leave," she hissed at Tabby. "You'll be ruined after today anyway and then Greg won't want anything to do with you. I am just sorry I won't be here to see it."

"If you do anything to ruin Tillie's wedding to further yourself, you'll answer to me," Tabby threatened.

"Have a nice day," Becky said, walking away, flipping a full tray of muffins off the table and onto the floor.

"Just let it go…just let it go," Tabby muttered to herself.

The caterer apologized over a and over again and promised that if

Tabby continued to use him he would clear all personnel with her first before hiring anyone. He hurried away to clean up the mess that Becky had made on the floor.

Tabby walked around snapping pictures of the reception hall that she could use for promotional purposes later. She grabbed the flowers out of the walk-in and left for the bride's house.

She arrived at the Twittle house to a barrage of questions. Tillie looked like she was about to burst into tears. Gladys was screaming at everyone about everything. Donald was trying to calm down his daughter while yelling at his wife to be quiet and go sit down.

The photographer and Tabby separated family members into several rooms for the different stages of the photo shoot. Things quieted down for a short while until Gladys started to complain about the number of pictures being taken and how expensive it was going to be.

Tillie seemed to be distracted during the photo session. She kept staring at the photographer like she knew him, but she didn't say anything. Tabby had hired the photographer, Trevor Upton, and he shouldn't have been known to any of the locals as he had just moved from the west coast to the east coast claiming he couldn't afford to live in California anymore. He was starting up his business again that he had left behind, and Tabby decided to give him a try after perusing his wedding portfolios. Tabby caught Tillie staring at him several times throughout the hour that they took pictures.

The photo session was finally finished at the Twittle house. Tillie and her sister, Beth, who was the matron of honor, climbed into the front limo while the rest of her family climbed into a second limo. They arrived at Cole's house twenty minutes before the service was to start. Tillie stayed in the limo until Cole was ushered out to the back yard so he wouldn't see the bride before the ceremony.

The sun was shining brightly as Tillie walked down the rose pedal covered aisle on her proud father's arm to her husband-to-be. The ceremony was short but sentimental; even Gladys cried as her daughter took her vows. The bridal party, Tillie's parents, and the bride and groom formed a receiving line at the back of Cole's yard. Tabby gave them explicit instructions that when the line ended they were to meet her in the front hall of the lodge and not to enter the reception area where the guests were seated.

Tabby hurried down the path to the reception hall. After a quick check around the interior she assured herself everything was ready for the incoming guests. She checked with the DJ to make sure he had the schedule of announcement that needed to be made.

The guests were arriving through the side door and finding their seats. The bar became a very busy place, but it only served juices, soda, and Mimosa as it was the drink of choice of the wedding couple to go with their breakfast theme.

The guests were asked to be seated. The wedding party was announced and entered to a large round of applause. Tillie was beaming as she walked to the head table. It was the first time in her life that she was the center of attention and she was enjoying every minute of her time in the spotlight. The bride and groom were served by their own private waiter. The rest of the guests were called, table by table, to fill their plates at the breakfast buffet. Tillie and Cole picked at their food and then decided to walk around and talk with their guests.

The matron of honor and best man stayed at the head table and ate. Jerry opened his jelly tray only to discover that he had blueberry and grape, neither of which he liked. When he thought no one was looking, he opened the groom's jelly tray which contained peach and strawberry. Jerry loved peach jam; it was his favorite. He slathered two pieces of toast, returned the tray to his brother's spot and inhaled both pieces of toast.

A little while later, Jerry started to feel hot and slightly dizzy. All he wanted to do was go outside and get some fresh air as he was having trouble breathing. No one saw him leave.

He walked around the parking lot and decided to go back to his brother's house to lay down; he was so sick that he didn't even think about his best man duties. He just barely made it into Cole's house and collapsed onto the couch. An hour later he was dead.

The reception continued without anyone noticing that Jerry was gone. It came time for the cake cutting and the champagne toast by the best man, but he was still nowhere to be found. Three times Cole returned to the head table and noticed his brother was still among the missing. His plate of food was still at his seat so Cole assumed that his brother had gone out for a smoke. He checked outside and in the bathrooms, but couldn't find Jerry anywhere.

"Where's Jerry?" Tillie asked.

"Knowing my brother, he probably got bored and left. He's like that," Cole said, shrugging. "We'll ask your dad to do the toast, okay?"

The reception passed quickly for Tillie who had never talked so much a day in her life. As the final dance was approaching for the newly married couple, they were standing at the head table looking over their plates and realizing they hadn't eaten a thing all morning. They decided to stop at a restaurant on the way to the airport in Boston.

The DJ called them out onto the dance floor for their farewell dance. Gladys cried for a second time that day watching her daughter and her new husband dance. Donald lovingly put his arm around his wife while brushing away a tear or two of his own. The music wound down and the bride and groom waved good-by to their guests and met Tabby out in the vestibule.

She told them the photographer was waiting outside Cole's house to take their pictures in their honeymoon outfits. At the end of the reception, Tabby would collect the wedding gifts, cards and wedding regalia from the head table to leave at Cole's house for their return.

Tillie hugged Tabby and thanked her repeatedly for a wonderful day. Cole and his wife walked out the door, hand in hand, ready to start their new life together. The wedding planner returned to the reception to make sure the morning finished smoothly.

People were already leaving as most of them were locals who had taken the morning off from their businesses to attend the wedding and had to get back to work. Tabby was packing up the items on the head table that needed to be taken to Cole's house so the caterers could clear the table off and start breaking down.

She heard a police siren coming from the direction of Cole's house.

Sheriff Puckett received a call on his radio and jumped out of his chair. He spoke to Deputy Small and Doc Holden and the two men hustled out the door. Next, the sheriff walked in Tabby's direction with a grim look on his face.

6

"You need to come with me," the sheriff stated. "Cole found his brother and he's dead."

"Where is the body?"

"They found him on the couch in the living room. We need to go now. You need to calm Tillie down while we do what we have to do," Sheriff Puckett insisted.

Donald Twittle cut them off before they managed to get out the door. He wanted to know what was happening and if his daughter was involved. The sheriff gave him a condensed version and told him he didn't want word to get out to the rest of the guests. Tillie's dad insisted on accompanying them to Cole's house. He told them he would meet them there after he after he made some excuse to Gladys without telling her what was really going on.

Tabby and Sheriff Puckett entered the back door into the kitchen. Tillie was sitting at the kitchen table crying. Cole was trying to comfort her and answer questions that were being asked of him by Deputy Small and the Doc at the same time.

Doc Holden walked back into the living room waving at the sheriff to follow him. The body was half on and half off the couch. Jerry's hand was clutching at his chest.

"It looks like he had a heart attack," Puckett commented.

"No, I'm afraid not. Look at the tint to his skin and fingernails; it's blue. This man has been poisoned," the doc stated firmly.

"Poisoned?" Cole asked, coming in from the kitchen. "Who would poison my brother? No one in this town knew him but me. Tillie didn't even know him until yesterday."

"Your brother's not from around here?" the sheriff asked.

"No, he flew in from the west coast for the wedding. He's the only family I have left…or had left," Cole lamented. "Who would do this?"

"Does anyone know when he left the reception to return to the house?" Doc Holden asked.

"The last time I saw Jerry he was eating his breakfast at the head table," Cole answered.

The others shook their heads in agreement.

"Clark, go back to the reception area and see if Mr. Brightman's dinner is still at the table. Bag it and anything else he might have eaten or drank," the sheriff ordered. "Doc, how long do you estimate he's been dead?"

"I would say no more than two hours," Doc stated.

"So, is it safe to say he was poisoned at the reception somehow?"

"I can't say for sure until I do an autopsy and see the contents of his stomach," he replied.

Donald Twittle walked to the living room door and surveyed the area around him. He had just left his daughter in tears in the kitchen and demanded to know what was going on.

"Donald, Doc thinks that Jerry Brightman has been poisoned. We have a real problem," the sheriff stated. "We don't know where he was poisoned; at the wedding reception or here."

"You don't think Cole or Tillie had anything to do with it? They were at the reception the whole time?" Donald asked, listening to his daughter crying in the kitchen.

"No, I don't," he acknowledged. "But I can't let them leave for their honeymoon just yet."

Tabby came in from the kitchen and was listening to what was being said. Her mind popped right back to Becky Tillman and her threat to

Tabby about ruining her reputation. She brought up the conversation to the sheriff. He said he would talk to her as soon as he left Cole's house.

"Can I call the coroner to come get the body? I'd like to sit in on the autopsy and see it completed as soon as possible," Doc asked.

Clark returned with everything from the head table. Jerry's plate was bagged along with the other three plates, all the glasses on the table and the four silver jelly trays. The caterer confirmed that nothing had been removed from the table.

The coroner's wagon pulled into the drive-way. The body was loaded in the back, along with all the bagged evidence that had to be tested. Cole would have to go to the funeral parlor and sign the paper-work to have his brother cremated after they were done with the body and the funeral parlor would hold on to the urn until Cole returned from his honeymoon.

The sheriff gave the okay for the bride and groom to leave for the local bed and breakfast where they would stay until they were cleared to travel. Tabby went with Tillie to help her change out of her wedding gown and keep her calm. Cole changed out of his tux and loaded the two suitcases into his car.

The car had been plastered with just married signs and tin cans tied to the bumper. Everyone between Whipper Will Junction and Boston would know the happy couple had just been married; when and if they ever made the journey to the airport.

The photographer took their pictures getting into the decorated car. Tillie was still staring at him as her and Cole drove away.

7

No one noticed the figure that was hiding behind a tree on the far edge of Cole's property watching the happy couple as they drove away. Punching the tree out of anger, the figure hurried away.

Tabby and Donald Twittle walked back to the reception. Gladys rushed up to her husband wanting to know what was going on at Cole's house that the police had to be summoned. Samantha Moon, Tabby's mother, also joined the group.

"I don't want to discuss it here, Gladys," Donald said. "Wait until we get home."

"I demand to know what's going on," Gladys insisted.

"I SAID we'd discuss it at home," Donald said, taking her elbow. "Tabby, you did an excellent job. I have never seen my Tillie happier than she was today. Please bring the final bill to me at the antique shop."

"I will, Donald," Tabby confirmed.

He escorted his wife out of the building, the whole while listening to her yapping in his ear. Tabby turned to her mom. Samantha Moon owned *Mystic Happenings* on the south end of town. A hippie, who never left the era of the sixties, she was still snickered at behind her back even though she had lived in the town among the locals for over twenty-five years.

"What is going on?" her mom asked.

"Cole's brother is dead," Tabby answered, looking around to make sure no one was close to them. "Doc thinks that he was poisoned."

"Really? Who around here even knew him?" Samantha asked. "Wasn't he from the west coast?"

"Yes, that's what makes it strange," she answered.

"Unless, it wasn't supposed to be Cole's brother that died," her mother commented. "There were four people sitting at the head table. Has anyone else got sick in the reception hall?"

"Not that I know of," Tabby replied. "Please don't say anything to anyone about the poison aspect of his brother's death. I don't think the sheriff wants that information released to the public until it's confirmed."

"I won't say anything; my name isn't Gladys Twittle," her mother snickered.

"I have to run. I need to collect all the gifts and cards and bring them to Cole's house. I'll talk to you later," Tabby said, kissing her mom on the cheek.

"That ring that you are wearing is a real sparkler. When will it be my turn to be mother of the bride?" Samantha asked, teasing her daughter.

"You're impossible," Tabby said, smiling and evading answering the question.

"I just hope I live to see it happen," her mother stated, clutching her heart area.

"Bye, Mom," Tabby chuckled, waving and walking off.

Why is everyone in such a hurry to get me married off? The only one who doesn't push me about it is the one that I am getting married to. Becky's probably hoping that Greg and I never get married.

She picked up the wishing well that was full of wedding cards to bring to her car.

"It was a beautiful wedding and reception, Tabby," Judy Montgomery, owner of the *Whipper Will Diner* said as she passed the wedding planner at her car. "I've never seen Tillie so happy."

"She was happy, wasn't she?" Tabby agreed.

"I just hope whatever happened at Cole's house didn't spoil her day," Tom Montgomery said. "They are both okay, aren't they?"

"Yes, they are on their way to *The Sparrow Bed and Breakfast* as we speak," Tabby smiled. "They will be in the Caribbean soaking up the sun together very soon."

"Good for them," Judy said. "Where was Greg? I didn't see him at either the wedding or the reception."

"He had two weddings that his shop was doing the flowers for today and he couldn't get away," Tabby answered.

"That's too bad," Tom said. "I mean that's good for his business, but not for his social life."

"Well, back to work we must go," Judy stated. "I actually enjoyed having a morning off; it doesn't happen very often."

"We'll see you tonight for supper," Tabby said as they walked away.

Tabby's car was stuffed to the roof with wedding gifts. She took the top layer of the wedding cake, the topper and boxed them up to put them in Cole's freezer for the couple's one-year anniversary. Tillie's bouquet was placed back in its original packaging for transport to the house.

The photographer returned to the hall to check in with Tabby. He told her that he would have the proofs ready in two weeks and drove off. She watched him leave still curious as to why Tillie kept staring at him.

She checked with the caterer to make sure that she was not needed any more. He assured the wedding planner that he would take care of the clean-up, still trying to get back in her good graces after the Becky Tillman mess-up. Tabby left the reception hall, happy that the wedding had gone so well.

Sheriff Puckett was still at Cole's house along with Deputy Small. She entered the house leaving everything in her car. The living room still contained the yellow tape sectioning off the area where Jerry died.

"Sheriff Puckett, is it okay if I bring in the wedding gifts and pile them in the den off the living room. I promise to stay away from the yellow tape," Tabby requested.

"That's fine. We're done here for now. Do you have a key to lock up?" the sheriff asked.

"Cole gave me an extra key before he left," Tabby answered.

"Do you want some help?" Deputy Small asked.

"That would be great," Tabby replied.

While bringing the gifts in, Tabby wrestled with her conscious on whether or not she should tell the sheriff about the conversation she heard between the two brothers prior to the wedding. She decided that she better be up front with him if she wanted to keep his trust in the future. As they made the last trip into the house, she told the sheriff what she had overheard.

"I don't want to get Cole in trouble, but Jerry sounded like a real jerk," Tabby said.

"You didn't hear Stephanie's last name or where they were married?" the sheriff asked.

"No, it was never mentioned," Tabby insisted.

"Okay, we'll check it out."

The last of the gifts were placed in the den and Tabby stuck the cake in the freezer in the kitchen. They locked the house and left.

Tabby returned to *Jellies, Jams and Weddings* at one o'clock. The shop was hopping with tourists and Janice looked wiped out. Thelma was ringing up sale after sale at the register, smiling and talking with everyone, not at all phased at how busy they were.

"Do you want to go to lunch? Tabby asked Janice as she darted by her.

"Do I ever!"

"Go, get out while you can," Tabby instructed her employee, laughing.

For the next hour while Janice was gone, Tabby waited on customers and stocked shelves. She was setting finished gift baskets on the front shelves when she spotted a gathering outside of her store. Everyone was standing just to the right of the front window of her shop. She decided to go out and see what was going on.

8

"She would definitely tell you to use my bakery for your wedding cake," Tabby overheard as she walked out the door.

"I really hope you're not lying again and referring to me in that last statement that you just made," Tabby demanded.

Becky Tillman turned and glared at Tabby as she approached the gathered group on the sidewalk. She stood two feet away from Becky and crossed her arms over her chest.

"Don't mind her, she's just cranky because her boyfriend is spending more time with me than her. You need to come into my shop and sample my cake flavors and make your own decision. Here's some coupons for a free taste testing; pass them around," Becky insisted, ignoring Tabby.

"Becky, get out from in front of my shop," Tabby stated in as level a voice as she could muster.

"I'm not in front of your shop; I'm to the right of your shop in front of the alley," she retorted. "Besides, it's a public sidewalk and you can't tell me where I can stand or not stand."

Tabby turned to the crowd, which had got even bigger when the two women had started to exchange words.

"Let me address her first statement. I do not endorse her bakery. I use *A Slice of Heaven* located in Larsen and I am very happy with their work," Tabby started to say.

"Seriously? You make your clients go all the way to Larsen when they can walk to my shop?" Becky threw right back at her.

"Second," she said, holding up her left hand and flashing her diamond ring around so that everyone could see it. "She doesn't spend time with my boyfriend. We are happily engaged and just because her shop is next door to his shop she thinks in her twisted little mind that she spends more time with him."

"Happily; yea, right," Becky snorted. "Take your coupons and come see just how good my baked items are. Judge for yourself who is telling you the truth."

Tabby pulled out her cell phone and dialed Sheriff Puckett's number. Then, she disconnected the phone without Becky knowing that she had done it.

"Sheriff Puckett, would you please come to my shop? Becky Tillman is here causing problems, *again*. You will, thank you. See you shortly," Tabby said, tucking her phone in her back pocket and smiling at her foe.

"She said again," one of the women whispered to her friend.

"I don't need your coupon, thank you," another woman said, handing her coupon back to Becky and hurrying off.

"You'll pay for this," Becky warned as she threw the remaining coupons that she was holding up in the air and stomped off.

"I don't think I'll be going into her bakery," another woman told Tabby. "She seems to be a real trouble maker. You hold on to that fiancé of yours; don't let her win."

"I will, don't worry," Tabby said, smiling. "Have a great day."

Tabby walked back into her store to see all her customers watching what was going on through the front window. Janice had come back from lunch and was also there watching.

"Are you okay?" Janice asked.

"I'm fine. Don't anyone worry about a thing. It's all taken care of," Tabby assured all the onlookers. "Who wants to try a sample of my peach jam, which just happens to be my jam of the month?"

The customers left the front window and followed Tabby to the small round table set up next to the register. She passed out little white spoons and let people sample her peach jam. It paid off as fourteen jars flew out of the store after the tasting.

"Nice save, boss," Janice whispered, opening another case of peach jam to put on the shelf.

"I am so glad that tomorrow is Sunday and we are closed," Tabby stated. "I have so much cooking to do, but first, Greg and I are going to the estate sale at the Piper house. There's several pieces he was interested in purchasing."

"It's so weird that the state can just walk in and takeover everything because Betsy Piper went to jail," Janice stated. "I heard the house is going to be auctioned off next month."

"That's the word around town," Tabby confirmed. "I wish I had the down payment they are requesting to bid on the house. That place is awesome and it's still close enough to town to walk to work."

"Maybe the reward money that you are supposed to be getting for finding the stolen bank money will come in so that you can bid on it," Janice commented. "You did fill out the paperwork almost six months ago."

"That would be great, but I don't even know how much the reward is that I'm getting."

"Well, you were getting two of them; one from the bank and one from the insurance company. You would think that the two combined would be enough for a down payment to be able to bid on the house," Janice replied.

Just prior to Christmas, Tabby had discovered the location of money that had been stolen in a bank robbery many years ago and was never recovered even after one of the robbers had been caught and sent to jail. The rewards that had been posted back then were still available for anyone who recovered the money and turned it in to the FBI. She had filled out the necessary papers and filed them in January.

"I filled out the paperwork so long ago that I am not going to hold my breath waiting for the money," Tabby said. "Insurance companies take their time processing things when the money is going out and not coming in."

"True…" Janice mumbled.

"Hey, does someone want to drive an old lady home; it's almost closing time?" Thelma piped up from the register area. "Normally I'd walk, but these old bones are really aching today."

"I don't see any old lady around here, do you Janice?" Tabby asked, smiling.

"Nope, me neither," Janice answered, looking around the shop.

"Okay, you two. Who's taking me home?" Thelma asked.

"Go ahead, Janice. I can take care of the last fifteen minutes by myself," Tabby stated. "I'll see you both on Monday."

There were only three customers left in the store at closing time. Tabby rang their sales up and locked the front door. The town was quiet for the beginning of June. Then, she remembered that there was a public barbeque out on Fuller's Point at six o'clock. She had gone last year, but it took her almost two hours to get off the point as there was so much traffic and only one way in and out. She decided to pass on the event this year. Fourth of July was coming and there would be a big town celebration for that holiday that Tabby and Greg would attend together.

The cats met Tabby at the top of the stairs. It was that time of year that the tourists descended on Whipper Will Junction and the cats had to remain in the apartment instead of being free to wander the shop. Happy to see their owner, they followed her everywhere.

While Tabby dressed for supper, the two cats wrestled on the bed. Ghost fell off, claws sunk into the bedspread, pulling it to the floor. Freeing himself from the fallen bedspread, he took off down the hallway with Marmalade chasing right behind him.

"How can two cats cause so much trouble?" Tabby yelled down the hallway at her furry roommates, picking up the spread and returning it to the bed.

"Anyone home?" Greg yelled.

"I'll be right out."

"Where's Buchannan?" Tabby asked as she entered the living room.

"I brought him home. He seemed out of sorts today at the shop. He went right to his bed and closed his eyes when we got to the house," Greg answered, patting Ghost.

"Are you going to bring him to the vets tomorrow and have him checked out? He is older, and the least little thing could make him sick," Tabby replied.

"We have a ten o'clock appointment," Greg said. "The vet agreed to see him even though it's Sunday."

"Good. I hope he's okay, Tabby said. "He seems so happy when he's at the flower shop."

"And my customers love him," Greg added. "I'm going to go to supper and then go right home to see how he's doing."

"Are you still going to the estate sale tomorrow?"

"It depends on what the vet says, I guess. It doesn't start until noon so there is a chance I can still go," Greg answered.

"Why don't we go to supper and then go check on Buchannan together. I can walk home from your house and that way you can stay with him," Tabby suggested.

"Sounds good to me," Greg said, opening the door. "You ready? I'm starved."

"You're always starved," Tabby laughed, locking the door behind her.

The diner was chaotic, but the couple finally found two seats at the long counter to eat supper. As they were enjoying a little quiet time together, Becky entered and plopped herself down on the stool that had been vacated next to Greg.

"Hi, Greg," she said, smiling, totally ignoring that he was with Tabby.

"Hi, Becky," Greg answered, always being the gentleman.

She picked up her menu and spread it open to read, making sure her arm was up against Greg's.

"Unbelievable!" Tabby announced loudly. "What part don't you understand that Greg is my fiancé and that you need to back off and go away, Becky?"

"It's getting awfully loud in here, don't you think, Greg?" Becky asked, sweetly.

"Look, Becky; you need to stop this. Tabby and I are going to be married. You need to find someone else to center your attention on and leave us alone, please," Greg told her.

"You're not married yet, are you, Greg?" Becky asked, standing up. "I'll see you around."

She tossed her menu at Tabby and walked out the door.

Tabby picked up the menu to wing it back at Becky, but Greg grabbed her arm and took the menu away from his fiancé.

"Don't sink to her level," he said, laying the menu down on the counter.

Then you tell me what we are going to do about her," Tabby asked out of frustration.

"Nothing," Greg answered.

"What do you mean nothing?" Tabby demanded.

"Just what I said; nothing. If we ignore her, she will eventually get bored with her little game and go away," Greg explained.

"I don't have your tolerance," Tabby insisted, picking up her mocha frappe.

"She really knows how to push your buttons, doesn't she?" Bea asked, as she set their bill face down in front of them.

"That's putting it mildly," Greg muttered. "She just won't take no for an answer."

"All she's doing is making herself look like a fool," Tabby stated.

"Says the one who was just going to wing a menu at her," Greg commented.

"I wonder why she came to this town of all places," Bea said. "She's not from here and as far as I know she has no family here. I think she said that she came from California when she was in here one night."

"Another one from California," Tabby muttered.

"Oh boy, I have to go. Gladys Twittle wants her tea," Bea said. "She will probably question me on what happened over here so that she has something to talk about at the coffee shop in the morning."

"Please, don't say a word to her, Bea," Tabby requested. "I've had my fill of her gossiping ways already."

"My lips are sealed," the waitress promised as she hurried off.

"What did you mean by your last comment?" Greg asked.

"Which one?"

"Another one from California," Greg answered.

"It just seems that we are getting flooded with people moving here or visiting here from California," Tabby stated.

"Like who?"

"Well, there's Becky, and the photographer that I hired for Tillie's wedding had just moved back here from California. And let's not forget that our dead best man was visiting from California," Tabby answered. "Don't you think that it's kind of weird?"

"Yea, I guess," Greg shrugged. "Are you almost done? I want to get home and check on Buchannan."

"I'm done," she said, finishing her last French fry.

"Greg paid the bill, they waved goodbye to Bea and left for Greg's house. They unlocked the door and looked around. Buchannan would usually be at the door, tail wagging to greet Greg.

"Where is he?" Tabby asked, concerned for the dog.

Greg headed to the living room. The dog was laying on his bed watching his owner. His tail thumped on the floor, but he never raised his head up off the bed. He was too weak to move anything but his tail.

"Tabby, call the vet," Greg requested, tossing her his cell phone.

Tabby stepped into the kitchen to talk to the vet while Greg sat on the floor and placed Buchannan's head in his lap. He talked quietly to the dog all the while stoking his head softly.

"Doctor Keeger said he would be right over. He's was on his way home and said he'd swing by to check out Buchannan," Tabby informed Greg.

Tabby stood near the front door waiting for the vet to arrive. Greg stayed with Buchannan. Tabby watched him with the dog. She could tell that Greg was hurting inside worrying about his furry friend. The vet arrived, and Tabby showed him to the living room.

Doctor Keeger checked the dog over. His face was telling the whole story.

"I think that Buchannan was older than we thought when you first adopted him, Greg. Truthfully, I don't think he will make it through the night," the vet said quietly. "I'm so sorry."

Greg didn't say anything at first. Finally, he thanked the vet for coming and asked him what he owed him for the house call.

"It's on the house; don't worry about it," Doc Keegen stated. "I'll check in with you tomorrow."

The vet left. Greg looked at Tabby.

"I know what has to be done," he said, looking lovingly at his dying roommate.

9

"What are you talking about?" Tabby asked.

"If Buchannan is going to die, I want him to die where he is the happiest," Greg insisted. "We need to take him to the flower shop."

"What can I do to help?" she asked.

"Grab me a couple of blankets from the hall closet. Then, can you pull the car up to the front door, please."

Greg wrapped the dog in a blanket and carried him to the car. He held the dog while Tabby drove to the flower shop. He turned on the lights and propped opened the front door of the shop. He moved Buchannan's bed closer to the front door. He set the dog on his bed and sat on the floor next to him.

"I want people to come in and say goodbye," Greg said quietly, stroking the dog's head.

"Why is the front door open? Aren't you supposed to be closed this time of night?" Sheriff Puckett asked, poking his head inside the door.

Greg didn't answer, so Tabby made a motion to the sheriff that she would meet him outside. She followed him out and explained that Buchannan wasn't going to make it through the night and Greg wanted him to be where he was the happiest, around people.

"I can help," he said. "I'll go to the diner and the Brown Bear Lodge and pass the word that Buchannan needs visitors here at the shop. We'll give him an awesome send-off to the Rainbow Bridge."

The sheriff left, and Tabby returned inside. She told Greg that Sheriff Puckett was going to round up some visitors for Buchannan. Greg smiled, shook his head and continued to stroke his beloved pet. Tabby wandered around the shop and finally sat down on one of the fountain benches so that Greg could have his privacy with the dog.

People started to trickle in; most of them locals who knew the dog from visiting the shop. They sat on the floor with Buchannan, patted him and told Greg how sorry they were that he wouldn't be at the shop anymore. In a short amount of time, the dog had made many friends.

At first, Buchannan's tail would thump on the floor with each visitor. He kept his head in Greg's lap, his eyes closing in a needed rest in between visitors. As the time passed, his tail wagged less and less.

The sheriff returned and sat on the bench with Tabby.

"I haven't had much of a chance to talk to you since Tillie's wedding. We got the lab results back," he stated, watching Greg and the dog.

"Did you find out how Jerry ingested with the poison?"

"Yes, we did. I don't think it was meant for best man," he answered. "The poison was in the peach jam in the groom's jelly tray."

"Are you saying that someone wanted to poison the groom, Cole Brightman, instead?"

"That's what it looks like," Sheriff Puckett answered. "Unfortunately, we have a lot of questions to ask him. I don't think Tillie's going to be a happy camper when he has to explain about his past wife."

As Tabby started to say something a loud commotion came from near the front door. Becky Tillman had rushed into the flower shop and plopped herself down on the floor next to Greg.

"Oh, Greg, I am so sorry to hear about Buchannan," she lamented, reaching for Greg's hand. "Is there anything I can do to help you?"

"Are you kidding me?" Tabby grumbled.

"I'll take care of this," the sheriff said, standing up. "You stay here."

The sheriff walked over to Becky and told her to follow him to the front door. He explained that this was neither the time or the place for her to be here and that Greg should be left alone to spend what little time Buchannan had left to be with his dog. She started to argue with the sheriff and he sternly gave her an order to leave the shop.

She stormed out the door as several more people came in to say good bye to the dog. An hour had passed, and people were still coming into the shop. During one of the lulls, Buchannan looked up at Greg and wagged his tail. There was so much love in his eyes for the person who had taken him in and rescued him from the shelter.

Greg told him how much he loved him and continued to softly stroke his head. Buchannan laid his head down in Greg's lap, let out one last sigh and crossed over the Rainbow Bridge into the arms of his previous master.

The sheriff closed the front door and locked it. He walked back over to Tabby and they sat quietly on the bench while Greg mourned the loss of his friend. People continued to walk up, looking through the window and then walking away when they saw Greg on the floor with the dog.

A short time later, Tabby sat on the floor next to Greg, putting her hand on Buchannan's head.

"He loved you, you know," she stated. "You gave him his life back; the life that he loved, here at the shop with people."

"I know. I just thought that he'd be around longer than he was," Greg admitted. "He was such a goofball. Did you know that he loved toothpaste? I can't count how many tubes that he bit through and squished out all over the house."

"You'll see him again, someday," Tabby said.

"I don't even have anywhere to bury him," Greg whispered. "I don't own my own house so that I have a yard to keep him safe."

"You can bury him in the back of my mom's shop, *Mystic Happenings*. It borders the cemetery and she owns the property. It will be passed on to me, so it will be kept in the family and Buchannan will always be safe there," Tabby suggested, trying to ease Greg's worry.

"Really? You don't think that she would mind?"

"I think that she would insist on it."

"I'll help you bury him in the morning if you'd like," the sheriff offered, walking up to the couple sitting on the floor. "You're going to need a deep hole to keep the coyotes away from him."

"I'd appreciate that," Greg answered.

"Good, I'm going to head out. I'll call you in the morning to find out what time to meet up with you," Sheriff Puckett confirmed. "And, Greg, I'm really sorry about Buchannan. I'm going to miss him greeting me at the door with his ball."

"I'll lock the door behind you," Tabby offered, standing up.

The sheriff left, advising some late visitors that the dog had already passed as he walked away from the flower shop. Greg wrapped Buchannan in the blankets that he had been laying on. He placed the blanketed dog into the smaller walk-in cooler that was off the back-room work space.

"Come on, I'll walk you home," he said to Tabby. "I need some fresh air."

He locked and alarmed the flower shop. The couple walked hand in hand towards Tabby's apartment totally unaware that they were being watched by Becky as they left.

10

It was Sunday morning and Tabby was busy cooking jelly on her only day off. It was right in the middle of tourist season and the shop had been extremely busy. Her mind kept wandering to how Greg and Sheriff Puckett were doing burying Buchannan. She had called her mother the previous night when she got home and received her approval to bury the dog on the property.

Tabby had two batches done and was starting on the third when Greg came through the door. He was dirty from head to toe.

"Can a guy get a cup of coffee around here?" he asked, plopping in a kitchen chair.

"Let me make a fresh pot. Everything go okay?"

"Yea, Buchannan is buried deep enough that the coyotes will never find him. We put a couple of big stones that were on the edge of your mom's property over the hole to protect him even more. He's buried right up against the fence to the cemetery."

"I'm glad that it's done. I'll start the coffee in a minute," she said, stirring the batch of jelly on the stove.

"I'll get it," he said, walking towards the coffee pot.

"Are you still going to the estate sale today at the Piper house?"

"I think so. I really want that turn-of-the century mahogany bookcase. I wouldn't mind getting the matching hall tables that go with the bookcase either."

"That bookcase is huge. Where are you going to put it if you buy it?"

"I may have to lay it down in the spare bedroom until I buy my own house. It definitely won't stand up in the rental that I am in right now."

"It looks so beautiful in the den at the Piper house. It's too bad that my reward money hasn't come in yet. I would have loved to bid on the house when the state auctions it off next month. The house is gorgeous," Tabby stated. "Then the bookcase could stay right where it is."

"Don't you think it's a bit creepy living next to a cemetery?" Greg asked, pouring his coffee.

"I think it's kind of cool. Why? Would it bother you?"

"I guess not. I think the beauty of the house would outweigh the fact that it is next to a cemetery. You really like that house, don't you?"

"Yes, I do. It's just too bad that I don't have the money to pay the deposit up front to even place a bid on it. The house is so old and has so much character. There is nothing else like it in this whole area," Tabby admitted.

"Do you want to go to the estate sale with me?" Greg asked.

"It starts at noon, right?"

"The preview time is a half an hour earlier. They are giving people a chance to walk around the house and make a list of what they want," Greg answered. "Will you be done with your jelly by then?"

"I will. This is the last batch for today," Tabby claimed, shutting off the stove and reaching for her heat resistant gloves so that she could hold the hot jars to fill them with the sweet mixture.

"As soon as I'm done with my coffee, I'll go home and shower. I'll be back to pick you up at eleven-fifteen," he said.

"Sounds good to me. Maybe I'll find something that catches my fancy, too; just not as big as your choice of items," she said, laughing.

Ghost wandered out from the bedroom and spotted Greg sitting at the kitchen table. He jumped up in his lap and started purring. Marmalade sat on the floor watching her brother.

"You're the only one he's friendly with," Tabby said, watching the cat turning inside out to get Greg's attention. "I can hear his purring all the way over here."

"We're best friends, aren't we, Ghost?" Greg said, patting the cat and drinking his coffee.

"Yes, you are," Tabby confirmed.

"I think I'm going to take my coffee with me. I'll be back in a while," Greg said, standing up and putting the cat down on the floor.

"I'll be ready," Tabby said, turning a filled jar upside down to seal it.

She finished her jellies and placed the jars on a table in the spare room to cool down. Tabby changed into a simple sundress and matching sandals to accompany her fiancé to the estate sale. She sat in her recliner, enjoying a cup of coffee and watching the cats wrestling in the sunbeam coming in the front window.

Greg poked his head through the back door.

"Are you ready to go?"

She patted the cats, told them to be good and left the apartment with Greg. They had decided to walk because the day was gorgeous and they each needed the exercise.

Was there anything that interested you in the house?" Greg asked, reaching for her hand as they walked.

"Truthfully, I didn't notice much when I was in there last time as I was a little busy trying to catch a killer. I'm glad they are giving people a little time to look around and check the listed prices," Tabby admitted.

"I'm going to check out the books when we get there to see if there are any older books that I might be interested in adding to my collection. I already know I want to get the bookcase and matching tables," Greg said. "I'm hoping that no one else is interested in them because of their size."

They arrived at the house to see cars parked up and down the entire length of Ball Road and people standing around everywhere waiting to be let in for the preview.

"Man, I didn't think it would be this busy," Greg whispered. "There's even cars from out of state here. The bank must have advertised this sale everywhere."

"There are a lot of antiques in the house. Most of the furniture was already there before Mrs. Piper even bought it," Tabby whispered back. "I wonder how many people are really here to see the inside of the house knowing that it's coming up for auction next month."

Samantha Moon, Tabby's mom, walked up to her daughter and gave her a hug. Dressed in her normal attire of a long-ruffled skirt and pheasant top, love beads and a peace headband holding her waist length, straight grey hair down flat, she captured people's stares as she walked among them. A genuine hippie, she had become accustomed to ignoring other people and lived happily in her own little world.

"Mom, what are you doing here?" Tabby asked.

"There are some display cases in the basement that I am interested in for my shop," she answered.

"You've been down in the basement?" Tabby asked.

"Oh, yes, many times. Mildred kept all her ghost hunting items down in the cellar so that no one would see them. I delivered many special orders to her house in secret."

"I didn't realize that you were friends with Mildred Piper."

"We weren't friends, really. We just went ghost hunting together on occasion," her mother answered. "I did visit her ghost at the library the other day. I told her she had to move on, but I don't think she's going anywhere soon. She's as stubborn dead as she was alive."

"They're opening up," Greg announced.

There was a mad push to get through the front doors. Even though it was just a viewing session, there were certain buyers that had to be the first ones to get in the house. Several people started pushing and people were falling to the ground and getting trampled on. Sheriff Puckett had to come out of the house to stop the trouble before someone got hurt. One man was escorted off the property because he wouldn't keep his hands to himself.

Greg, Tabby and Samantha finally made it in through the front door. Greg went to the den to see if anyone was checking out the bookcase and no one was near it. The books had been cleared out of the bookcase and loaded into six boxes to be sold as one unit. If Greg wanted the older books, he would have to buy the whole lot. He figured that he could give whatever books he didn't want to keep to Jenny to sell in her bookstore.

Samantha disappeared downstairs to check out the display cases. She was also hoping to pick up some of the stock that she had sold to Mildred Piper so that she could resell it in her shop, *Mystic Happenings*.

Tabby was standing in the living room perusing the contents of the room when she was bumped rather hard from behind. She turned.

"Oh, I'm sooooo sorry," Becky Tillman said, smiling.

"No, you're not. Stay away from me today and stay away from Greg. DO you understand me?" Tabby demanded.

"Oh, Greggy is here?" I'll have to see what he wants to buy and maybe I can buy it for him as a gift," she said, wandering off to find Greg.

Tabby stormed forward to go after her, but Sheriff Puckett grabbed her by the arm.

"Don't do it. She's only making a fool of herself acting like she is. From what I hear around town, her business has dropped off to almost nothing because of her reputation," the sheriff stated. "Just ignore her, as hard as that may be."

"She is so infuriating," Tabby stammered.

"I know, but you have to rise above it. Tillie and Cole will be leaving tomorrow for their honeymoon. I left a message on his phone to come and see me before they leave."

"Tillie is going to have a fit when she finds out about Cole's first wife," Tabby said, frowning.

"I know; I was thinking that you have such a calming affect on her that you might consider being at the station when they come in?"

"Sure. I'll be at the shop so just give me a call when you need me," Tabby answered.

"Great. I'm going to finish looking around. My wife loves those enamel eggs that are in the hutch over there. I might try to get those for her collection," the sheriff smiled. "Stay away from Becky."

"I will. I'm going to find Greg. I'll talk to you tomorrow."

Tabby wandered into the kitchen to see Greg talking with an older lady that had a name badge on her lapel. She was one of the associates that worked for the company that was handling the estate sale and the house auction. They were deep in a discussion, so Tabby did not want to interrupt them. Becky on the other hand, pranced right up to them and started talking over their conversation.

Stay away; just stay away like the sheriff said to. Greg can handle her.

Greg looked at Becky in total disbelief. The woman that he was talking to stopped in mid-sentence and stared at Becky in disgust. She didn't notice the looks and kept talking. Greg grabbed her by the elbow and led her to the back door. Tabby followed at a short distance.

"Becky, I have tried to be nice to you. I have told you that you need to back off as Tabby is my fiancé and we are getting married, but you won't listen. Now, I am telling you for one last time. Stay away from me and Tabby. I don't want you within fifty yards of me. Do you understand this time?" Greg said in a loud enough voice that everyone was watching them.

Becky looked around and saw that she had an audience.

"Oh, Greg, all I wanted you to do was love me," she lamented. "But, she had to come between us. Someday we'll be together; I can wait."

"You are unbelievable," Greg yelled, losing it. "Stay away from me, stay away from my shop and stay away from Tabby. I don't know how to make it any clearer to you."

"I do," Tabby spoke up. "How about a restraining order?"

Becky turned and glared at Tabby. She took several steps in her direction and Greg quickly stepped forward and stood between them. The sheriff came in from the living room and felt the tension that was building in the room. The auction associate quickly stepped forward in Tabby and Greg's defense. Sheriff Puckett escorted Becky out of the kitchen and out the front door advising her not to return. She flipped her hair over her shoulder and walked away.

He returned inside after making sure that Becky was not coming back. The sale was just starting. People were hustling around trying to pick up the things that they wanted. The sheriff ran to the hutch and scooped up the three enamel eggs that he wanted to buy for his wife.

Greg was first in line and bought his bookcase, tables and boxes of books. Once he had those items purchased, he was more relaxed walking around and checking out other things.

Tabby had ascended the stairs and was more interested as to what the upper rooms contained. She entered the first bedroom and noticed that the secret room that they had found last time they were there had been closed off.

"Pretty nice house, don't you think?" came a voice from behind her.

She turned to see Trevor Upton, the photographer, standing in the doorway.

"I came to see if they had any items that I could buy to use as props for my photography studio. I saw you heading up the stairs and wanted to tell you that Tillie's proof sets are coming out beautiful. If you like I can drop them off at your shop when they are done," he said. "Nothing much left in this room, is there?"

"That would be fine," Tabby answered. "No, there isn't."

"I've walked around. It's mostly bedroom furniture and sheets and stuff."

"Thanks for the info, but I think that I'll take a look around anyway," Tabby stated.

"Okay. Well, have a good day and I'll see you around," he said.

"Tabby! Are you up here?" Greg called out as he passed Trevor in the hallway.

"I'm in the first room," she answered.

"Find anything interesting?" Greg asked, entering the room.

"No, this room is empty. Want to go look in the other rooms with me?" she asked, taking his hand.

They investigated each bedroom and their contents. Many of the upstairs rooms had boxes of household items that looked like they had never been unpacked when the Pipers moved in. Three of the eight upstairs rooms had bedroom sets in them.

One room, the master bedroom, had a beautiful mahogany four-poster bed with all the matching pieces. It was a king size bed that looked like it had seen little use.

"This is stunning," Tabby said, breathlessly. "The set looks like it was made for this room."

Greg walked over to look at the price tag that was hanging from one of the finials on top of the posts. The tag had two different listings; one price for the entire set and on the other side, prices for all the individual pieces.

"I think that this set was already here when Mrs. Piper bought the place. It just doesn't look like her taste in furniture if you compare it to the pieces downstairs," Tabby observed.

"This set is really old," Greg stated, opening the bureau. "All the drawers have dovetails joints and they are made of a different kind of wood than the rest of the piece."

"So, now you are a furniture expert, too?" Tabby laughed.

"No, I just have a lot of old pieces at my grandmother's Victorian house. Pieces that, I might add, would look incredible in this house," Greg answered.

"Do I get the feeling that you are falling for this house like I already have?' Tabby smiled.

"Maybe, maybe not."

"You are, just admit it." Tabby insisted.

"I love the matching mahogany fireplace in this room. It looks like it was designed to match the bedroom set, or the other way around," Greg said, running his hand over the mantel piece. "This whole house is an architectural masterpiece."

"Do you like the bedroom set?" Greg asked, turning his attention to his fiancé.

"It's gorgeous, but I don't think it would fit in my second-floor apartment," Tabby said, wistfully. "I do believe that it was meant to stay in this house, in this room, and stay a permanent piece of the history here."

"That's what I thought, too," he admitted.

"I'll be right back. I have to find a bathroom; too much coffee this morning," Greg said.

"I'll be in the next room checking things out," Tabby stated.

Tabby entered what must have been Betsy Piper's room growing up. Dolls and toys were shoved in the corner that had been pulled out of the closet. Twin beds with matching bureaus and night stands filled the smaller room. There hadn't been much of an area for Betsy to play in as a child. A jewelry box sat on the top shelf of the closet. Tabby reached up to take it down and when she did she tripped over a doll that had been left on the closet floor. She fell forward and. her shoulder hit the back wall. A small door slid open revealing a rolled piece of parchment that had been stashed behind it.

Setting down the box, she picked up the paper and unrolled it. Greg had entered the room and she hadn't even noticed.

"What did you find?" he asked, looking over her shoulder. "Wow!"

11

"This is incredible," Greg stated.

"Do you think that they are the original blueprints for this house?" Tabby asked.

"The print is dated 1802 so I would have to assume that it is original," Greg answered turning it over. "But, I think that the original house has been added to over the years because what we are standing in is much larger than what the blueprint shows."

"Do you see what I see? Greg asked scrutinizing the paper in front of him.

What?"

"The fireplace doesn't match up with what is drawn," Greg stated, looking at the mahogany fireplace in front of them.

"What are you two up to?" Tabby's mother asked as she entered the room. "No good probably."

"Look what Tabby found in the wall," Greg said, waving his future mother-in-law over to them.

"What do you mean...in the wall?"

"I tripped and banged my shoulder into the back wall of the closet and a door slid open," her daughter answered.

"Only you," her mother mumbled. "What did you find?"

"In my opinion, it looks like the original blue prints of the house. It's dated 1802," Greg answered.

"Why would someone hide it?" Samantha inquired, looking at the hole in the closet wall.

"I don't know, but it sure makes this house just that much more interesting. I so wish that my reward money would come in so that I could bid in the auction to buy it," Tabby said.

Greg and Samantha looked at each other and smiled. They were up to something of their own that didn't involve Tabby and she had no idea that Greg was plotting to bid on the house without her knowing. They stopped smiling as Tabby started to turn around to face them.

"What do you think that you should do with the blue prints?" Samantha asked.

"I want to take them with me, but that would be wrong," Tabby admitted.

"I think the right thing to do would be to put them back in their hiding place and just keep quiet about it. Maybe, the new owners will find them sometime in the future," Greg stated.

"I guess you're right. There is just so much history here to be learned that I hate to just leave them for the next owners to hopefully find," Tabby grumbled.

"Let's put them back and figure out how to close the sliding door before someone else comes in here and sees it," Greg suggested, gently pushing Tabby towards the closet.

Greg replaced the blueprints in the hole and they felt around the wooden wall until they found the tiny notch that Tabby had hit to open it. It quietly slid closed and its secret was once again hidden. Tabby stood staring in the closet.

"Come on," Greg said. "There are other rooms to check out."

The three of them walked around and picked up a few more things here and there to purchase. Tabby found a matching set of hurricane lamps that were trimmed in gold leaf and painted with bunches of lilacs. Greg found another bookcase to purchase that had been hidden behind some mattresses that were standing up against a wall in one of the back bedrooms.

When they paid for their additional purchases, Greg made arrangements with the auction house clerk to pick up the larger furniture pieces that he had already purchased in the coming week. Samantha would return the following afternoon with Greg's van to remove the display cases from the basement. Sheriff Puckett and Deputy White had volunteered to help her move them to her shop.

Samantha gave her daughter a hug and said goodbye. Greg and Tabby walked back to her apartment, each one carrying a lamp up Main Street.

"Do you want to eat an early supper at the diner tonight" I have to be in Larsen for a five-a.m. flower pick-up and I'd like to be in bed by ten. It's been a long day," Greg announced.

"How about I cook some burgers on the back deck and we just relax for the rest of the day?" Tabby asked. "That way we don't have to fight the tourists for a table at the diner."

"Sounds good to me," Greg agreed.

The couple sat on the back deck soaking up the warm June sunshine. The small round grill had been fired up and they were enjoying ice cold beers as they waited for the coals to come up to temperature to cook the burgers.

They had stopped at Mac's Market and picked up some potato salad from the deli and four ears of fresh corn on the cob.

The cats meowed at the inner screen door to be let out. Tabby kept telling them no and they finally gave up and disappeared in the house. Greg was quiet. Tabby knew that he was thinking of Buchannan, so she left him with his thoughts and went in to husk the corn and shape the burgers for the grill.

Several minutes later, Greg called for her to come to the back deck. A middle-aged man in a three-piece suit accompanied by a smartly dressed young woman were standing with Greg.

"Tabitha Flower Moon?" the man asked.

"Yes, I am Tabitha. May I help you?" she answered.

"My name is Clifton Smith. My client is Carol Brightman; Jerry Brightman's wife," he stated.

"I didn't know that Mr. Brightman was married," Tabby said.

"Mrs. Brightman was in California waiting for her husband to return from his brother's wedding," he stated in response to her statement.

"I'm so sorry about her husband's death," Tabby said.

"This is a packet outlining the law suit that I have filed on behalf of my client against you and your business in the wrongful death of Jerry Brightman," Smith said, holding out some folded papers for Tabby to take.

"What? You can't be serious?" Greg said, stepping forward and taking the papers.

"You'll see that I am quite serious," he stated firmly.

"Jerry Brightman was murdered. I had nothing to do with his death," Tabby protested.

"It was your jelly that killed Mr. Brightman," he replied.

"Over one hundred and fifty people ate jelly that day. How can you hold me responsible for someone else putting poison in one certain container?" Tabby inquired.

"Save it for court, Miss Moon," Smith demanded. "Unless you decide to settle out of court as outlined in the documents."

"I will never settle out of court. That would be admitting that what happened was my fault," Tabby insisted. "I'll see you in court, Mr. Smith. Now, kindly leave."

"I will be in touch," Smith said, turning to leave.

"No, the only person that you will be talking to from now on is Miss Moon's attorney," Greg said, reaching in his wallet and handing Smith a business card.

"Very well, if you have decided to make this more difficult than it has to be," Smith announced. "I will discuss anything further with your attorney."

He walked down the back stairs without another word. As he walked to his car, Tabby noticed a woman sitting in the front seat watching everything. She turned her face away when she noticed that Tabby was staring at her.

That must be Carol Brightman.

Tabby plopped down in her chair and reached for the papers that had been delivered.

"I didn't know that you had your own personal attorney," she said, half smiling.

"With my parent's and grandmother's estates, I had to have an attorney that I could trust. Joe will know what to do and if he feels he can't handle this case he will advise me as to someone who can," Greg informed her. "Don't worry; this is just someone that's looking to make a fast buck. They won't win, Tabby."

"I wonder if Cole knows that his brother was married. And, how did they find out so fast that Jerry was poisoned?" Tabby pondered.

"It's just one more thing that the sheriff will have to ask him," Greg reasoned. "I think that you should tell Sheriff Puckett about this lawsuit and see what he thinks."

"I'll talk to him tomorrow," Tabby said, folding the papers back up and tossing them on the patio table. "I can't believe that this is happening. I mean, I have insurance, a million in and a million out, but I never thought that I would ever have to use it."

"Let's not think about it anymore until we talk to Joe and see what he says," Greg advised. "Let's get those hamburgers cooking."

Tabby returned to the kitchen to finish preparing the food. She made the patties and dropped the corn into the already boiling water. Greg came in and took the burgers for the grill. He gave her a hug and told her not to worry as he could see the concern that was still on her face over what had just happened. She gave him a weak smile and went back to making the salad.

They ate their meal, mostly in silence, as Tabby couldn't get her mind off the lawsuit. Greg left shortly after they were done eating, promising to call his attorney when he got home.

Tabby went inside and made herself a cup of tea. She pulled out her laptop and did a search for Clifton Smith. There was fourteen Clifton Smith's scattered around the country, four of which were lawyers. One was in California, one in Boston and two in the Midwest. She went to the individual sites and only one had a picture; the attorney in Boston was not a match.

Her cell phone rang; it was Sheriff Puckett calling. He told her the meeting with Cole had been set up for ten o'clock the next morning. Tabby told him about the lawsuit and he told her to bring the documents with her and he would check things out using his connections. She hung up and returned to sipping her tea while watching the cats playing.

This lawsuit couldn't come at a worse time. Her business was just becoming established and showing a profit and she had nine more wedding contracts that would take place over the next twelve months. If word got out, how many of the brides would back out on their contracts? This lawsuit could ruin her wedding business never mind that the jelly, her jelly, had been served containing poison. How many people would shy away from buying and eating her jelly if that information was released locally?

People knew that Jerry had died at Cole's house and just assumed that something had happened there. Only a handful of people knew that the jelly had been poisoned at the wedding. .

Then, another thought hit her. What if Becky Tillman found out? She could destroy Tabby and her business like she had threatened to do. This was just the kind of thing that Becky would use to wreck Tabby's life.

Her thoughts were interrupted by her cell phone sounding again. It was Greg who said that his attorney would be coming from Larsen the following day to look over the lawsuit paperwork. He would meet with them at two in the afternoon at Tabby's shop. He agreed with Greg that it sounded like an attempt at easy money, but would know more when he could read over the paperwork himself. Greg said he would see her at two.

Tabby tried to watch television, but found her mind wandering so much that she zoned out for large chunks of the show. Giving up, she went to bed.

She opened the shop the following morning at eight. Janice and Thelma were both manning the shop when she left a few minutes before ten for the sheriff's office. She entered the station to see Tillie and Cole sitting on the wooden bench outside of Sheriff Puckett's office. Tillie rushed up to her looking anxious.

"Tabby, what is going on?" she asked. "Is Cole in some kind of trouble?"

"Why don't we wait for Sheriff Puckett? He'll tell you everything," Tabby assured her, knowing she wasn't going to be a happy camper when she found out about Cole's first wife.

The sheriff came out of his office and called the three in closing the door behind them.

"Have a seat, please," he requested, returning to his seat behind his desk and opening a file folder.

"Cole, I don't know any other way to tell you this except to come right out and tell you. We found the source of the poison that killed your brother. The poison was not meant for him, it was meant for you," the sheriff stated. "It was in the groom's jelly tray in the peach jam."

"That is my favorite flavor of jam," Cole confessed. "Jerry's, too."

"Someone was hoping that you would have eaten the peach jam had you spent any time at the head table," the sheriff insisted. "Jerry had his own jelly tray and there was no poison in it. It was definitely meant for you."

Tillie started to tear up and took hold of Cole's hand. Tabby sat quietly watching them both.

"Who would have wanted Cole dead?" Tillie asked.

"Does the name Stephanie mean anything to you?" the sheriff asked Cole.

He hung his head and didn't answer.

"Do you mean the same Stephanie Baker that Cole was married to years ago?" Tillie inquired.

"You know about Stephanie?" Tabby blurted out.

"Yes, Cole told me all about her and their marriage."

"Then you know that they were never legally divorced?" the sheriff asked.

"I do know that she disappeared without a word and after trying to find her for three years, Cole finally gave up," Tillie answered. "It's been over ten years since she left."

"Cole, did you ever file for a divorce when Stephanie didn't come back?"

"No, sir, I didn't. I had the documents filled out, but never went to court to finalize it. Isn't there some kind of law that says after so much time has passed, you're not married anymore?"

"I think that varies from state to state. That was something that you should have checked out prior to marrying Tillie," the sheriff suggested. "I would suggest that you look into the answer to that as soon as possible."

"Yes, sir, I will. Do you think that this has something to do with Stephanie?"

"We don't know. It is something that we are looking into," the sheriff answered.

"Sheriff, please don't let this get out. My mother will go nuts if she learns about this; you know how she is. Please give us some time to straighten the matter out and if we can, no one needs to know about Cole's previous marriage," Tillie pleaded.

"Yes, I do know how your mother is. My problem is, Tillie, that it is your husband who was the real target of the poisoning and we have to find out why and who did it. His past may be made public during the investigation," the sheriff stated. "I think you both should be ready if it does. Are you sure you have no idea what happened to your first wife, Cole?"

"Sheriff, I don't have a clue. I thought we were happy, and then one night she went out with her two sisters to the local bar and never came home again," he answered, tapping his foot on the wooden floor.

"Can you or Tillie think of anyone who would want you dead?" the sheriff inquired. "Do you have any enemies?"

"I don't even have any friends here except for Tillie," Cole answered.

"I need you and your wife to make me a list of everyone that you know or have had any contact with recently. Someone tried to kill you and I don't want them to have a second chance to get it right," Sheriff Puckett warned.

"Cole, did you know that your brother was married?" Tabby asked.

"Jerry and I weren't that close, but I think he would have told me if he got married. Why?"

"It seems his wife from California has stepped forward and is filing a lawsuit against Tabby and her business for the wrongful death of her husband," the sheriff answered. "He never mentioned to you while he was here that he had a wife back home?"

"No, he didn't. Why wouldn't he have brought her with him for the wedding? It doesn't make much sense if you ask me," Cole commented.

"You brother never referred to a woman named Carol?" Tabby insisted.

"No, never."

"As a matter of fact, Jerry told me at dinner the night before the wedding that he would never fall into the trap of marriage. He said that he was engaged at one time, but she demanded too much of his time and he needed his freedom," Tillie announced. "Cole told him that our relationship wasn't like that and Jerry said every marriage was like that and laughed."

"Interesting," Tabby mumbled.

"Okay. Thank you for coming in and answering my questions. Both of you need to be extra careful until we catch who killed your brother. If you think of anything else, please call me right away," the sheriff admonished. "Get me the lists of names as soon as you can."

"Can we go home now? I'd like to open some of our wedding gifts," Tillie asked.

"Yes, we are done processing the house. If you receive any kind of food as a gift, don't eat it," the sheriff suggested. "Put it aside so that we can test it before you consume it. Right now, you can't trust anyone."

Cole and Tillie left, but Tabby lagged.

"What's on your mind, Tabby?" the sheriff asked.

"Everything that they said would point to the fact that Jerry Brightman wasn't married. Why would he run his mouth like he did, but still have a wife?"

"Some guys are just guys. They talk big when the other half isn't around because they can't when they are," he answered.

"Do you do that?" Tabby asked.

"Not me," he chuckled. "The way this town is, I couldn't say a single word that wouldn't get back to the wife."

"So, you think that he figured he was safe talking that way because his wife was in California," Tabby asked.

"Could be," the sheriff shrugged. "I'll find out exactly where his brother lived and check to see if a marriage license was ever issued to a Jerry and Carol Brightman anywhere near that area."

"Thanks, I appreciate any help I can get. Greg's attorney is coming from Larsen this afternoon to look over the papers that were delivered and counsel me on what should be done," Tabby stated.

"Greg's attorney? He sure takes good care of you," Sheriff Puckett smiled. "Don't do anything to screw up and lose that guy."

"I won't, believe me," Tabby assured him. "No matter how hard Becky tries to make that happen."

"Is she still causing problems?"

"Every chance she gets. If word gets out about this lawsuit, she will have a field day at my expense," Tabby groaned. "That reminds me; how many people knew that the poison was in the jelly?"

"Not many. Just myself, my deputies and the people in the coroner's office. The cause of death was listed as homicide by poisoning on the death certificate, but there was no mention of the jelly. Why?"

"Because Carol Brightman's attorney specifically stated that he knew my jelly killed her husband," Tabby answered.

"Her attorney could have called the coroner's office to get the information," the sheriff stated. "One of the clerks could have released the information about the jelly without realizing they shouldn't have."

"That's true," she frowned. "Oh, well, back to work while I still have a work to go to."

"Think positive, Tabby. We'll get this whole messed straightened out, I promise."

"The sad part is that they offered me a figure to settle out of court. They assumed that I would just roll over and automatically pay them to save my business."

"Don't you dare pay them a cent," the sheriff ordered.

"I wasn't going to. I told the attorney that I would see them in court and he didn't look very happy about it."

"I'll be in touch when I find out anything to help you," the sheriff stated.

Tabby walked back to work not knowing much more than she did when she got there.

12

Greg arrived at two o'clock with his attorney. The threesome went upstairs to Tabby's apartment to have their conference in private. Tabby made a pot of coffee and her and Greg waited in silence while Joe looked over the documents.

"Okay," he said, setting down the papers and picking up his coffee mug. "The first thing I have to do is verify the marriage. I also want to check on her attorney and verify his license. Did he say where he was from?"

"No, he didn't. He didn't even give me a business card to be able to get in touch with him. He said that he would call you," Tabby answered.

"His name and number are on the letterhead, but it doesn't look like a California listing. It looks more like a cell phone number," Joe stated. "Did they at least say where they were staying?"

"No, but there is only two bed and breakfasts around here; not a lot to chose from," Greg said, refilling his coffee mug.

"I'll check them out. Tabby, I don't want you to talk to these people; no communication at all. I will be the only one to converse with them. Do you understand?"

"Yes, I understand."

"This is a serious situation. They are asking a huge sum of money here, not only in court but as an out of court settlement as well. Greg tells me that you like to investigate and solve mysteries. You can't do that here; you have to leave everything up to me," Joe said, frowning. "You could do something to jeopardize the case that could result in a loss."

"She'll keep her nose out of it, won't you Tabby?" Greg confirmed.

"I said that I would," she insisted.

"I have my work cut out for me. I'll be in touch as soon as I know anything," Joe said, collecting the papers and putting them in his briefcase. He shook Greg's hand and was shown out the back door of the apartment.

"I have to get back to the flower shop," Greg said, setting his mug in the sink. "Please, try to curb your mystery solving ways and let Joe take care of it. I don't want them to win on a technicality."

"I promise, unless of course something just happens to fall in my lap…" Tabby mumbled.

"TABBY!"

"I'm joking, geez." she said, batting her eyes in Greg's direction.

"I'll see you for supper," he said, not amused, closing the door.

Tabby returned to the shop downstairs. Janice greeted her with a warning.

"Don't look now, but Gladys is waiting for you at the bridal table," Janice whispered to her boss. "She wouldn't leave."

"I got it, thanks."

Gladys gave Tabby the evil eye as she approached the table. Tabby wanted to laugh as she got closer to the woman who was dressed from head to toe in yellow. Her dress had daisies with crazy faces on them against a green background. Her hair had been died bright yellow to match the center of the daisies.

"What can I do for you today, Gladys?"

"I want, no, I demand a portion of the money back that we paid for Tillie's wedding," Gladys stated.

"And why would I do that?" Tabby asked. "On what grounds do you think that you deserve a refund? I fulfilled my contractual obligations."

The customers that were wandering the shop stopped to listen as Gladys was not the quietest speaker there was.

"I heard around town that you have a lawsuit filed against you for Cole's brother's death. I feel, in my opinion, that Tillie's wedding was compromised and did not run as smooth as it should have," Gladys said, even a little louder now that she had an audience.

"There was not a moment during Tillie's wedding that did not happen exactly as it was supposed to. Her wedding was perfect and Tillie herself would tell you that," Tabby argued. "And where and who did you hear about a lawsuit from?"

"I don't have to tell you my sources," Gladys insisted.

"No, but you will have to tell a judge when my attorney sends you a summons," Tabby said, getting in Glady's face.

"You wouldn't dare!" Gladys exclaimed, standing up.

"Watch me," Tabby threatened.

"You're just changing the subject so that you don't have to pay me back any money," Gladys retorted.

"I'll tell you what, Gladys. I will talk to Tillie and see if she feels that her wedding was compromised in any way by Cole's brother's death. If she does, then I will work something out with your husband as repayment. If she was satisfied, then I will tell Mr. Twittle she was and that will end it."

"You don't have to involve my husband in this," Gladys said.

"Just what I thought; Mr. Twittle has no idea what you are trying to do, does he? I think I will go talk to him right now," Tabby said, walking towards the door.

"Never mind…forget the whole thing," Gladys said, hurrying by her to get out the door first.

"How did she get wind of the lawsuit?" Janice whispered.

"I don't know," Tabby said, frowning. "But, I need to find out."

Tabby took a couple of steps and stopped. She turned around and walked into the back room with Janice right on her heels. Thelma came out from behind the register and started to socialize with the customers that remained in the store to get their minds off the scene that just played out in front of them.

"What are you doing? Aren't you going to go after Gladys?" Janice asked.

"I can't," Tabby answered.

"What do you mean you can't?" Janice demanded.

"I promised the attorney to stay out of it and let him handle everything," Tabby muttered. "I need to call Greg."

"Okay, I've just never seen you back down from anything or anyone. That does sound like the smart thing to do though," Janice admitted. "It makes me mad that Gladys is going to think that she won when you don't go after her."

"I'm more curious as to how she found out about the lawsuit," Tabby stated. "I only was served yesterday afternoon and I don't think that the attorney is going to run around town blabbing about it."

"How else would Gladys have found out about it then?"

"I wouldn't put it past her to have called the coroner's office, but she wouldn't have learned about the lawsuit there," Tabby said, taking out her cell phone. "I'm going to call Greg so that he can call the attorney and stop this from spreading any more than it has already."

"I'll be out on the floor stocking the jelly," Janice commented.

Tabby called her fiancé and told him what had happened. He promised to call Joe right away and hopefully, the attorney was still in the area to pay a visit to Gladys. Greg promised to let her know if he heard anything.

She sat in the back room, her hands tied, and she didn't like the feeling of being so helpless and relying on someone else. There was only an hour left until the store closed for the day. Tabby decided to spend the time decorating for the Fourth of July which was only a week away. Gram always told her that when she was down; decorate.

Red, white and blue streamers were strung around the store while silver, red and blue star bursts were hung in the front windows. The store looked festive by closing time. Janice left to drive Thelma home and Tabby finished locking up. She happened to glance out the window and noticed that Becky was standing across the street staring at her. Tabby walked out the front door.

Becky managed to cross the street in between the busy summer traffic on Main Street. She stopped a few feet from Tabby and smiled; and kept smiling while she continued to stare at her.

"Aren't you the happy one?" Tabby said nastily. "What do you want, Becky? I'm not in the mood for your foolishness today."

"Oh, are you having a tough week?"

"No different than usual," Tabby answered, not letting the obnoxious woman get to her.

"That's not what I heard. I told you I would end up with Greg if I just stayed patient. How does it feel when everything's not going your way?" Becky gloated.

"You've been listening to Gladys at the coffee shop too much," Tabby replied.

"I don't have to go into the coffee shop to know what's going on around town."

"And what is going on around town Becky?"

"Word is that you will be out of business soon; that you will be ruined. Lawsuits can be devastating. Let's see if Greg wants to stay with you then," Becky stated. "Things happens, bad things, when you take someone's life."

What Becky didn't know was that Greg and his attorney, Joe, had quietly walked up behind her. She was so busy harassing Tabby that she had no idea that they had been standing a few feet away for a good portion of the conversation.

"And how do you know about the lawsuit?" the attorney asked her from behind.

Becky almost jumped out of her skin. She knew that she had run her mouth way too much. She panicked for a moment, but quickly regained her composure.

"Answer the question Becky," Greg demanded. "Who told you about the lawsuit?"

"I don't remember. I …ah…heard it around town somewhere," she stammered.

"Where and from who?" Greg persisted.

"I told you, I don't remember. I have to go," she answered, brushing past the two men.

"We'll see you in court," Greg's attorney stated.

"And I don't care if Tabby's dirt poor, we are still getting married," Greg yelled.

"Oh. nice touch, Mr. Stone," Tabby commented as the attorney chuckled.

"Sorry…it just kind of came out," Greg mumbled.

"It's okay. It's nice to know that you would love me no matter what," Tabby said, smiling and taking hold of his hand. "So, what do I owe the honor of this visit?"

"I tried to pin Gladys down on who told her about the lawsuit, but she reused to tell me. Her husband even took my side and told his wife to tell me what I needed to know," Joe said.

"Gladys can be quite frustrating sometimes," Tabby admitted.

"That's all right. It's nothing that a subpoena to court can't take care of," the attorney said. "It would have been so much easier if she had just told me who told her."

"Are you ready to go to supper? Joe is going to join us," Greg informed her.

"Not quite. I got sidetracked by Becky and haven't finished closing the store yet. I need to feed the cats as well," Tabby said. "How about I meet you there in twenty minutes?"

"Sounds good. It may take us that long to get a booth," Greg agreed.

Greg and Joe walked up Main Street, stopping for a few seconds in front of Gladys' shop, *Penny Poor Antiques*. She didn't know if they were checking to see if Gladys was still there or if they were trying to spook her into telling them who released the information on the lawsuit by staring in the window a bit. She watched them until they walked out of sight.

She emptied the register and locked up the shop. The cats were anxiously awaiting their supper and as they ate Tabby set the deposit bag with the days receipts in the kitty litter bag under the bathroom sink. She quickly changed into jeans and a tank top, grabbed her purse and left by the apartment's back door.

Tabby exited the alley and walked at a leisurely pace towards the diner, enjoying the warm summer night. She passed by the many tourists that were walking Main Street, smiling and returning hellos that were offered to her. It was then that she saw Becky Tillman hurrying down the alley next to her bakery.

I know I am supposed to stay out of the investigation, but...

13

Tabby ran down the adjoining alley and stopped at the end before it spilled out into the rear parking lot. She wanted to look around to see if Becky was anywhere in sight because she didn't want to get caught spying on her. There was no sign of the baker or anyone else, so she figured that she must still be in the alley.

Tabby crept up to the opening of the alley that she had seen Becky go down, being careful not to show herself. She stopped at the corner of the building when she heard two people arguing. Becky was having a heated discussion with a male, whose voice sounded somewhat familiar to Tabby.

"You just had to run your mouth, didn't you?" the male voice asked.

"I'm just trying to stir up trouble like you asked me to do," Becky answered.

"Stirring up trouble is one thing, but leading people right to us is something else," he insisted.

"I didn't do that," Becky said. "Tabby is so busy trying to keep me away from Greg and now the lawsuit that she's facing, she can't think straight."

"I hope you are right. Now, our timetable needs to be moved ahead. You know what you have to do next, right?"

"It will be taken care of, believe me," she answered.

"Are you sure that you can handle it? You know the consequences if you don't."

"I can handle it. You just worry about your part," she demanded.

The voices ceased. Tabby ducked down behind some trash barrels that were in front of her in case they came out the back entrance to the alley. She was hoping they would so that she could see who Becky was arguing with, but no such luck. After a minute passed, she peeked down the alley, but they were gone.

She hurried up the alley, looking both ways before she exited. As she walked up to the bakery she could see Becky inside, waiting on customers at the counter. Now, it was Tabby's turn to put the pressure on Becky. She entered the bakeshop and stood in line waiting her turn.

Becky spotted her coming through the door and frowned. Her whole demeanor changed towards her customer. Tabby ignored her and looked around the shop while she waited in line. Baking school certificates lined one wall with Becky's name plastered on all of them. The other wall contained pictures. Some of who looked to be family and others of famous people who must have visited a previously owned business and autographed pictures for her.

Her turn finally arrived, and she was not greeted in a friendly manner.

"What are you doing here, Tabby?" she growled.

"I decided, that in all fairness, I have never tried your baked goods and that's what I am here to do now," Tabby explained.

Yea, right," Becky said, rolling her eyes. "Why are you really here?"

"If you don't want me to buy your baked items to sample and to stop shooting down your bakery, I'll leave," Tabby sighed, turning to leave.

"Fine. What do you want?" she said.

Tabby picked out a half a dozen different items. She tried to make pleasant conversation while Becky packed up her goods.

"It's nice that you stay open until eight o'clock for your working customers," Tabby commented.

Becky just stared at her, trying to figure out what her foe was up to. Tabby continued to smile, paid for her purchases and left the shop.

That ought to keep her guessing for a while.

She hurried to the diner knowing that she was almost an hour late. Greg and Joe were in the far corner booth nursing cups of coffee.

"Where have you been, or shouldn't I ask?" Greg inquired.

"I was walking over here, minding my own business when I saw Becky head down the alley next to her store. I knew if I came here to get you first we could miss whatever was going to happen," Tabby started.

"And…" Greg commented.

"I ducked down the next alley and listened to her and some man having an argument."

"Seriously, Tabby? Do you ever listen?" Greg muttered.

"If you had been caught it could have affected your case," Joe admonished.

"I know, but she looked mad and I knew something was up, so I followed her."

"The damage has been done. I'm not condoning what you did, nor do I want you to do it again, but what did you overhear?" the attorney asked.

"She definitely knows about the lawsuit. The man that she was arguing with was mad because he said that by running her mouth she had brought attention to them," Tabby answered.

"I wonder who them is," Greg pondered.

"I don't know, but it has been her job to keep me occupied by attempting to steal Greg," she said, continuing. "He said that they had to move their timetable up and then he asked Becky if she knew what she had to do next. She said she did and that was the last that I heard."

"Did you get to see who she was arguing with?"

"No, I didn't. They left by way of Main Street and were gone by the time I could look into the alley. His voice did sound somewhat familiar to me though," she replied.

"Tabby, you can't do this again. You have to let me take care of things according to the law," Joe advised. "You were lucky that you didn't get caught. Hopefully, no one else saw you listening in on their conversation; someone else that works with them."

"It just happened. I'm sorry. It won't happen again," Tabby insisted.

"Where have I heard that before?" Greg mumbled.

Bea walked up to the table with her order pad.

"Well, look who finally showed up. I need to get your order in to the kitchen; it's almost ready to close," she said. "Who's having what?"

They ordered their supper and while they were eating, Becky waltzed up to the take-out counter and ordered two meals to go. She didn't know that she was being watched as she sat on the stool waiting for her order.

"Two meals; that's strange. Becky lives by herself," Greg stated. "I have never seen anyone else go in or out of her house."

She picked up her bag and left the diner.

"I'm going to follow her. You two stay here. Tabby, I'll call you tomorrow," the attorney said, sliding out of the booth and throwing a twenty on the table for his supper.

He took off out the door in pursuit of Becky and her two meals.

"Joe didn't even finish his supper," Tabby stated, looking at the half-eaten plate of food.

"When this case is settled, I'll take him out for a nice steak dinner to make up for it," Greg replied. "What's the box on the floor at your feet?"

"Just some pastries," Tabby answered, brushing off the question.

"Pastries from where?"

"*Becky's Bakeshop*."

"You didn't go in there?" Greg asked, not happy at all.

"I may have. I just wanted to see what kind of mood she was in after her argument in the alley. And, I couldn't help myself by being nice to her to throw her off a little."

"Do you seriously want to lose this case? I thought the jelly shop meant a lot to you. Why are you doing such stupid things to risk everything that you have worked so hard for?"

"You don't have to be so harsh," Tabby complained.

"Not harsh, just truthful. You really need to think about what you do from here on out," Greg advised his fiancé.

"I guess you're right," she admitted, sighing. "I'll stay in my shop and let Joe do his job."

"That would be the smart thing to do," he replied.

They finished their meals in silence. Bea came to the table to ask about dessert, which Greg always ordered and devoured, but it seemed that he didn't want to stay around any longer than he had already. He paid the bill and told Tabby he would talk to her tomorrow. Greg was furious with her this time, she could tell.

"Trouble in paradise?" Bea asked, plopping her butt down in the booth.

"Greg is not happy with me right now. I did some stupid things that I shouldn't have done, and he let me know it," Tabby answered.

"So, quit doing stupid things," Bea answered smiling.

"I know; it's just hard to break old habits," Tabby replied.

"If you want to win this lawsuit against you, then you had better listen to your attorney's advice," Bea stated. "Keep your nose clean and stay out of the investigation."

"You know about the lawsuit, too?"

"The whole town knows about it. You don't think that once Gladys knew about it that it would stay secret for very long, did you?" Bea asked.

"I guess not," Tabby admitted. "I think I'll go home and hide with my cats. Say hi to Jen for me. I haven't seen her that much since tourist season started."

"I will. Keep your chin up. And between you and me; here's a tip for your attorney to check out. I saw Becky and that photographer that you used for Tillie's wedding driving out of town the other day heading toward Larsen."

"Bea, you're awesome," Tabby said, hugging her second mother.

She hurried home and did what she was supposed to do. She put in a call to the attorney and told him what Bea had told her. Afterwards, she settled in for the night and watched some television. Her mind kept wandering to Greg and how mad he was. She hoped that she hadn't done something so stupid that it would drive a wedge between them.

She fell asleep in the recliner and didn't wake up until the next morning. The sun coming through the front window told the cats that it was time for breakfast and they, in turn, told their owner by sitting on her head and batting at her nose. She fed the vocal cats, made a half a pot of coffee and headed for her bedroom.

Her cell phone rang just as she was about to hop in the shower. Thelma was feeling under the weather. She asked her boss if it was okay if she stayed home. Tabby assured her that she needed to take care of herself first and foremost and that they would be fine at the shop until she felt better. Thelma told her she would call her tomorrow and let Tabby know if she felt well enough to come in to work and hung up.

Ghost and Marmalade were rolling around on the bed when Tabby came out of the shower. She missed their antics down in the shop during the day. When summer arrived, and the tourist season was at it's peak, the cats had to stay upstairs in the apartment so that they could not escape out the front door that was continually being opened and closed. The locals missed seeing the store mascots and were always asking how the cats were doing.

Tabby opened the store at eight. Gladys came running in as soon as Tabby unlocked the door.

"What's up, Gladys?" Tabby asked the Town Mouth, knowing that she was there to pass on some juicy tidbit of gossip.

"I guess that you haven't heard?" Gladys said, picking up a jar of jelly and turning it around in her hand.

"Heard what, Gladys? I don't have time for your nonsense," Tabby said, grabbing the open flag.

"*Becky's Bakery* has a For Sale sign in the front window," Gladys answered.

"She just opened her bakery. Why would she be selling it?" Tabby wondered out loud.

"Despite all the slander that you slung her way, her business has been doing very well. She IS a wonderful baker, you know," the woman wearing the loud, yellow daffodil dress stated. "Don't you feel just a little bit responsible for her giving up her business?"

"Is that what you came here for? Are you looking for a confession that you can pass around town to blame me for her business going under?" Tabby demanded.

"Well, if the shoe fits..." Gladys gloated.

"That's it! Get out! I have work to do. Goodbye, Gladys," Tabby said, assisting the nosy woman out the door.

"Now why would Becky be selling her bakery? Is this the next step that they were talking about in the alley?

"Why the frown, boss?" Janice asked, coming in through the front door. "Is there something wrong with the open flag?

"Oh… no," Tabby answered. "Did you know that Becky is selling her bakery?"

"I saw the sign in the window this morning; it's the first I knew of it," Janice replied.

"Thelma won't be in today. She's not feeling well and called me to let me know. It's just you and me today," Tabby said, heading for the door to go hang up the open flag.

"I'll take the register," Janice suggested.

It was a spectacular day for the beach. The temperature hung around ninety degrees and the sun was shining brightly. Good beach days translated into slow business days. Small rushes of business from people who didn't like the beach took place throughout the day. The mailman came around noon and delivered several registered envelopes with Tabby's name on them and not the store's name.

One contained a check for a deposit on a wedding in the Fall.

Obviously, this bride hasn't heard about the lawsuit yet.

The second envelope had a return address from a law firm in Larsen.

Not another lawsuit...I can't take much more of this.

The envelope contained a letter, two pages long, that had a five-thousand-dollar check made out to Tabby attached to the second page. The law firm represented the bank association that had posted the reward for the stolen money that Tabby had recovered. She was to sign the second page and return it to the law firm upon receipt of the check.

"Janice, finally, some good news," Tabby said, poking her face out through the curtains that hid the work space at the back of the shop.

"What's up, boss?" Janice replied, using one of her favorite lines.

Tabby waited for the customer to leave the register area and then she held up the check for Janice to see.

"Is that what I think it is?"

"It's one of the two rewards that I filed for," Tabby answered. "But, you have to keep it a secret with this stupid law suit that's pending against me. I'm sure they would love to get their hands on this."

"Does this mean that you can bid on the Piper house in the auction now?"

"No, unfortunately, the deposit is ten thousand dollars just to place a bid," Tabby frowned. "I don't know if I could bid anyway. If I got the house, they may try to take it away from me in payment if they win in court."

"What a mess," Janice commented. "Speaking of they; look across the street."

Becky was standing on the sidewalk, staring at the jelly shop.

"Is it me or does she look kind of sad?" Tabby asked.

"Yea, kind of, I guess," Janice admitted. "Maybe, she's accepted the fact that she will never have Greg to herself."

"When I was in her store yesterday…"

"Wait a minute; you were in her bakeshop?"

"Yes, I was. I was trying to be nice to her to throw her off her guard. I stood in line, waiting my turn, and it's almost like she was mad that I was there, but afraid at the same time. Does that make any sense?" Tabby inquired.

"Maybe she was mad that you were there, but afraid at the same time that you were going to start trouble," Janice suggested.

"I guess, but I'm getting one of my gut feelings that everything is not as it seems," Tabby said, watching Becky scurry away knowing that she had been spotted.

Sheriff Puckett came in the door as the two women were staring out the front window.

"Are my pants on backwards or something?" he asked, chuckling at his own joke.

"Oh, hi, Sheriff Puckett. No, we were watching Becky standing across the street," Tabby admitted. "We weren't staring at you."

"Is she giving you problems again? Do you want me to go speak to her?"

"No, it's okay. Just let it go," Tabby sighed.

"I haven't been in to visit for a while; you know, tourist season and all. I missed my daily cup of coffee," he said, heading for the back room.

"It's nice to know that you didn't miss us, only the coffee," Janice replied.

"Oh, I miss you, too," he said, inhaling the aroma of the coffee before drinking it.

"Tabby, I wanted to tell you that they isolated the poison used in the jelly. It was antifreeze. The jelly was saturated with it, but Jerry Brightman managed to get back to his brother's house before it over took him," the sheriff stated.

"Antifreeze? That's why Jerry didn't even realize that he was ingesting it," Tabby surmised. "The sweetness blended in with the peach jelly."

"We did some checking around. It seems a week before the wedding, *Hank's Garage* was robbed. Care to guess what was taken?"

"Antifreeze," Janice piped up.

"Why didn't Hank report it?" Tabby asked.

"He figured it was just the local kids and it was only two gallons, so he didn't think that it was worth reporting," he answered. "Hank has no security system at the garage so there were no pictures of who broke in and took it."

"Do you think it was someone local?" Janice asked.

"We're kind of leaning that way," Sheriff Puckett answered. "Whoever it was knew that there were no cameras at the garage."

"That includes most of the town. And, everyone and anyone had access to the Bear's Hall the day of the wedding. The jelly containers were filled early in the day and left on the kitchen counters prior to being placed on the tables. The back door to the kitchen was open for deliveries all morning," Tabby said.

"Don't forget," Janice started. "Becky was at the hall that morning bringing in her baked goods. She did say that you would be finished, or was it destroyed after the wedding took place."

"We are checking on Becky Tillman's past. So far, nothing out of the ordinary has popped up except for the fact that she moves around a lot," the sheriff replied. "Her mother and father died in an airplane crash when she was only eight. She lived with her aunt in Larsen until she turned eighteen and then she moved to California."

"How did she end up here?" Tabby wondered.

"Don't know, but we're still checking things out," he answered, refilling his travel mug. "Are you going to be open for the Fourth of July?"

"No, and thank you for reminding me. I have to put a sign in the window telling people that we will be closed," Tabby replied. "If Greg doesn't stay mad at me, I think we will be going to the parade and the fireworks together."

"Don't you do anything to screw things up with that fine young man," the sheriff warned her. "I don't know how many times I have to remind you."

"I know, I know, you've told me before," Tabby replied, rolling her eyes.

"I mean it. He's got to be someone special if he can put up with you and your ways," Sheriff Puckett smiled. "Your mother likes him, too. Samantha doesn't trust many people, but she sure approves of him."

"I'll keep that in mind," Tabby replied as Janice snickered.

"I'm going to run. It's almost lunch time and I have to go see what trouble Gladys is causing at *The Tilted Cup*. Stay out of trouble, both of you," he said.

"I love it; guilt by association," Janice yelled as the sheriff went out the door.

"Shall we order a couple of sandwiches and eat lunch here? Janice asked.

"Sounds good to me," Tabby answered, taking out a menu from *The Tilted Coffee Cup*.

Janice was putting on her coat to go pick up lunch when an ambulance went screaming by the shop, heading south, out of town.

"I wonder where that's heading?" Tabby commented.

14

"I'll be right back," Janice stated.

Tabby walked to the front door, looking out to see if she could see where the ambulance had stopped. It was no where in sight. She returned to the register to ring up a purchase for a customer. Sheriff Puckett's cruiser flew by the store in the same direction that the ambulance had gone in. She hoped that none of the kids had been hurt at the summer session of daycare at the elementary school.

The shop cleared out, but a few stragglers came in while the women ate their lunch at the bridal table. They took turns getting up and waiting on the customers. Tabby had just finished closing the register drawer when her mother and Sheriff Puckett entered the shop. Neither looked very happy. Tabby knew it was something bad if the sheriff had stopped and picked up her mother on the way in to the shop.

"What is it? What's happened? Did something happen to Greg?" Tabby asked, holding her breath.

"Greg is fine," her mother answered.

"Then what is it?" she asked again as Janice came and stood next to her.

"Thelma's gone. She had a stroke; a bad one," Samantha replied. "There was nothing they could do for her."

Tears welled up in Tabby's eyes.

Janice walked into the back room. Tabby could hear her crying. She had become very close to Thelma, working together as much as they did. It was Janice that gave her a ride home almost every night as Thelma lived less than a mile past where Janice lived in *The Starling Apartments.*

"She called me this morning and said that she didn't feel good. I should have gone and checked on her," Tabby sobbed.

"You didn't know," Samantha said, putting her arm around her daughter.

The three customers that were still in the store saw the grief unfolding around them and left with the promise of returning for their jelly. The sheriff thanked them on their way out.

"I have to go check on Janice," Tabby insisted.

Janice was sitting on the floor in the corner of the room with her knees tucked up under her chin. Her face was tear stained and her hands were shaking. She looked up at Tabby who had knelt beside her.

"She was like my grandmother," Janice whispered. "I never had one you know."

"Same here. I always turned to her after my own Gram died," Tabby said, sitting down on the floor next to friend. "I'm going to miss her terribly."

"Me, too. She was going to teach me to crochet this coming winter."

She taught me, you know. I can teach you if you want to learn."

"I do want to learn," Janice claimed.

"Do you remember the day that she was so upset when Agatha died?"

"I remember. She was sad because she was the only one left in her graduating class," Janice answered.

"I bet that right now, the three musketeers are heading toward the Pearly Gates together. Gram and Agatha were probably waiting for her with open arms. More than likely, they are dancing and whooping it up celebrating their everlasting friendship that has carried over into Heaven," Tabby assured her. "That's the way I am going to chose to look at losing Thelma here on earth."

"She probably is totally happy being with her best friends. That doesn't mean that I won't miss her… a lot."

"We both will. But, every time we hear someone singing, we can smile and think of Thelma singing around the store as she worked," Tabby said.

"Yes, she loved to sing," Janice reminisced.

"Come on. Thelma wouldn't have wanted us sitting on the floor crying over her passing. Besides, my mother is running the store right now and God only knows what prices she is charging for stuff," Tabby said, smiling and standing up. "You with me?"

"Yea, for Thelma," Janice said, wiping the tears away with the back of her hand.

The two friends came through the curtains to see Samantha talking to several customers. She was trying to explain the shelf life of the jellies and jams.

"I got this, Ms. M.," Janice said, walking up to the group.

"Thank you. Are you sure that you're okay to be working?"

"I'm good. Thelma wouldn't have wanted us to be sad that she is finally joining her two best friends in heaven," Janice answered.

Samantha walked over to her daughter and hugged her.

"You did good back there," she whispered. "I'm glad that Janice has you as a friend."

"What are they going to do with Thelma?" Tabby asked.

"I have to go to the funeral home and make her arrangements. I am her executer and health proxy, the latter of which she doesn't need anymore," Samantha answered. "Will you be okay if I leave?"

"I'll be okay; sad but okay. Let me know about the arrangements, please."

"It won't be anything fancy; she didn't want it that way. Cremation and a small memorial service at the church," her mother answered. "I'll let you know."

Janice was back on the register. She smiled a weak smile and waved at Tabby's mother as she left. They both put on brave faces for the remainder of the day. Several times, Tabby could hear Janice crying in the bathroom. She let her friend stay in there as long as she needed to and didn't say anything about her crying when her friend would finally come out.

Janice's boyfriend, Eric Seaver, stopped for a visit, unaware of what had taken place. He could tell that something was not right because of Janice's swollen and enflamed eyes. Tabby suggested to Eric that he take Janice somewhere for a nice quiet supper and she shooed her employee out of the shop early.

The next hour Tabby sat at the register waiting on customers that had come off the beach and were ready to shop. She was happy when five o'clock hit and she could lock the doors. She helped the remaining shoppers that she had locked in and patiently answered questions, one after another. Finally, at five-thirty, everyone was gone.

She cleaned out the day's receipts, shut out the lights and only then noticed how quiet the shop was. She ran her hand over Thelma's stool and the tears started. There would be no more singing to the customers, disciplining the small children that ran loose in the shop and seeing her smiling face that lit up the shop every morning when she came through the door.

The tears continued to flow in the private, quiet of the shop. Sometimes, Tabby felt closer to Thelma than she did her own mother. Her mother was a hippie; a hippie that didn't understand many of the things that Tabby thought and felt. Oh, she loved her mother, but there was something about talking to Thelma that would calm Tabby down and make her think before she acted. Thelma had been there for her since Gram died. Now, there was no one to talk to that didn't blame the government for everything.

Tabby decided that she was going to put the picture that they took at the Christmas Stroll of Thelma, Janice, Greg and herself standing near the Christmas tree up behind the register. Thelma had been the center of attention that night and that was how Tabby wanted everyone to remember her when they came into the shop. She set Thelma's stool in the back room and went upstairs to her apartment.

The cats met her at the door looking for their nightly attention. She fed them and then sat on the floor, drinking her beer and looking out the front window at the people walking up and down Main Street.

Life goes on, even if one life ceases.

One hour and two beers later, she decided to pick herself up off the floor. She hadn't heard from Greg or the attorney and she assumed that Greg was still angry with her. She was poking around the refrigerator looking for something for supper when she heard a noise at the back door. She looked out the peep hole, but saw no one.

Opening the door slowly, she looked around the deck and saw no one. She was about to go back inside when she spotted a piece of paper that had been taped to her door. In large red letters were the words HELP ME. She grabbed the paper and returned to the safety of her apartment.

She was studying the paper looking for clues, when a loud knock sounded on the door. Tabby almost fell out of the chair that she was sitting in. She raced for the door and flung it open hoping to catch whoever it was that left the note.

Greg was standing there with hands full of Chinese take-out, and a surprised look on his face that the door had been opened so fast.

"Sorry, I didn't mean to knock so loud. I had no available hands, so I had to use my feet," he explained. "Can I come in and put this stuff down?

Tabby stepped aside and let him in.

"Did you see anyone in the parking lot when you pulled in?" she asked.

"No, why?"

"This was taped to my door just before you got here," she said, holding up the paper.

"Help me?"

"Have you been out the back door today? How do you know that it wasn't put there earlier while you were working?" Greg asked. "It could be someone just joking around."

"Or it could have been Becky trying to distract me with something else. It might have been there all day, I don't know. It's been such a stressful day; I can't think straight."

"I heard about Thelma. I'm so sorry. I know that she meant a lot to you," Greg said, taking Tabby in his arms. "She was a wonderful human being; so happy all the time."

"I thought you were still mad at me when I didn't hear from you all day. I haven't heard from the attorney either," Tabby said, resting her head on Greg's shoulder. "I thought something had happened to you when my mother and the sheriff came to the shop because you hadn't called at lunch like you usually do."

"I was mad last night; furious even. But, that doesn't mean that I love you any less. I just don't want you to lose everything that you have worked so hard for. But, I can see that no matter how hard you try, you are going to be a magnet for mysteries. Case in point," he said, pointing to the paper that had been taped to her door.

"I'm either in the wrong place at the right time or they come to me," Tabby replied. "I can't help it."

"I know, but it doesn't make it any less frustrating," he insisted.

"That food smells so good. Can we eat?" Tabby begged.

"Sure. I had a busy day, too. That's the only reason why I didn't call you," he said, kissing her forehead. "I did get a call from Joe. He said that he tried to call you, but you didn't pick up."

"My phone was on the back table all day. I didn't hear it ring," Tabby replied.

"Joe followed Becky to the parking lot. She got into a white car with a thirty-something male and then something really strange happened."

"What?"

"Joe said that she put a mask over her eyes; you know, like one of the ones that you use to block out the light when you sleep. When the guy was satisfied that it was in place, they drove off. By the time Joe got his car out of the parking lot, they were long gone. He said that they turned left out of the diner, so they had to go to either Carson's Bend or Larsen."

"A mask? That is strange. I guess Becky wasn't supposed to know where she was going," Tabby surmised, pulling dishes down out of the cabinet. "But, that does explain the two meals that she bought."

"Maybe, or maybe she was going to sleep while he drove, and the oncoming headlights bother her," Greg added. "Who knows."

"Bea told me last night that she saw Becky and Trevor Upton leaving together on another occasion," Tabby stated.

"Who is Trevor Upton?" Greg asked.

"Oh, I forgot, you weren't at the wedding. Trevor Upton was the new photographer that I hired for Tillie and Cole's wedding. He just moved back here from California and is trying to resume his photography business. It's weird that they all came here from California at about the same time," Tabby said. "Except for Becky; she was here way ahead of the others."

"Did you tell Joe all this information?"

"Yes, I did. I called him last night when I got home. He said that he would have his investigator go to California and check out the stories. He said as of last night he couldn't find Carol Brightman's attorney listed anywhere as passing the bar, here or in California. He found other Clifton Smiths, but none that matched the age of this one here."

"Sound fishy to me," Greg said, shoving a chunk of teriyaki beef in his mouth.

"Remind me after supper to show you the pictures that I took of Tillie's reception hall. She said that I could blow them up and use them around my shop for promotional purposes. The place was really beautiful," Tabby insisted.

"And the flowers? I'm sure they were the best that you've ever seen," Greg said, puffing up his chest and patting himself on the back.

"Okay, the flowers were great, too," she admitted.

"Thank you, I'll tell the owner of the flower shop. I know him personally, you know."

"You want to hear something else that is strange?"

"What?" Greg asked, going back for seconds on the shrimp egg foo young.

"While Trevor was taking the wedding pictures, Tillie kept staring at him. I don't know if she recognized him or if it was something else. Even as Cole and she drove away, she continued to stare at him out the back window," Tabby answered.

"Tillie seems to trust you more than she does anyone else. Maybe you should be the one to ask her why she was staring at him," Greg stated. "I can't believe that I am going against everything Joe has told you and am encouraging you to do this."

"If it will make you feel better, I'll ask Joe's permission first," Tabby replied. "Although, I can't believe that Trevor is not a professional photographer. The proofs that he dropped off at the stop were gorgeous. He really knows how to capture the moment."

"Maybe, he really is a professional photographer, but does other things on the side," Greg suggested in a mysterious voice. "Maybe, dun-dun-dah…that's his cover story."

"Do you want another beer or a cup of coffee?" Tabby asked, laughing at Greg's rendition of a television narrator from the old crime shows that they watched together.

"Coffee sounds great."

"I'll make a pot and then show you the pictures of the hall. I transferred them to my computer," Tabby said.

As Tabby made the coffee, she watched Greg, who was staring off into the living room.

"It's still weird not having Buchannan around," Greg said, sadly. "He was only with me a short time, but I really miss him."

"Yes, he was a big, lovable baby. I think Ghost and Marmalade miss him, too. He's running around, happy and healthy on the other side of the Rainbow Bridge," Tabby assured him.

"Yes, he is. I'll see him again someday," Greg said, rinsing his plate and setting it in the sink. "So, let's see this stunning reception hall with the absolutely gorgeous flowers."

Tabby sat down next to her fiancé and started flipping through the photos. As they were viewing the buffet table area, Greg pointed to someone standing behind the bingo board curtain like he didn't want to be in picture.

"Who's that?" he asked.

"I don't know. Let's see if we can enlarge that area of the picture," Tabby replied.

"Isn't that a camera lens hanging right there below the curtain?" Greg asked, pointing to a black object in the picture.

"It looks like it," Tabby agreed. "Let's blow it up some more."

"Yes, that's definitely a camera lens," Greg stated.

"The only one that had a camera like that at the wedding was the photographer, Trevor Upton. Why was he there at that time of the morning? I wouldn't have even known that he had been there if I hadn't caught him in the picture," Tabby pondered out loud.

"You can't be sure that is was him; all you have is a picture of a bottom half of a photo lens," Greg said. "A lot of people bring cameras to weddings."

"True," Tabby sighed.

They perused the rest of the pictures trying to catch sight of anyone with a fancy camera, but that was the only shot that the mysterious person had been captured in.

"Now, I really need to aske Tillie about why she was staring at him," Tabby said.

Greg's cell phone buzzed. He checked the screen and saw that it was his attorney calling.

"Joe," he said answering the call. "I'm putting you on speaker phone. What's up?"

"I just had a package delivered to my office. It seems that Carol Brightman has had a change of heart and lowered her out of court settlement by half. The letter from her attorney states that she needs to get back to California as soon as possible to take care of her mother who has fallen sick. Can you say convenient?"

"Or, can you say that they are trying to get whatever they can before they have to disappear?" Greg added.

"Yes, my thinking exactly."

"Hi, Joe," Tabby added.

"What do you think of the counter offer of fifty percent less than the original settlement offer?"

"I say that I am not giving them a cent and that we will battle it out in court," Tabby answered.

"Good. That's what I was hoping that you would say. I'll send the answer back to them first thing in the morning. Be careful, because I believe we are dealing with a professional con team and they are going to get mad that you won't just flop over and agree to what they want."

"I don't just flop over for anyone," Tabby said, angrily. "I will be careful, though."

"I'll talk to you tomorrow when I receive their answer to my reply. Good night."

Tabby set Greg's phone down on the table in front of him.

"Pretty convenient, huh? For them to use the sick mother routine to tug at your heartstrings is pretty low. I wonder how many other people that that has worked on?"

"Well, it won't work on me," Tabby stated firmly. "Do you want some more coffee?"

"No thanks, I had better head home. I need my beauty sleep, you know," he said, snickering.

"I have to agree with you; not about the beauty sleep, but just plain sleep. With Thelma gone, I am a person down in the shop. It will be just Janice and myself until I can hire someone," Tabby replied.

"I promise that I will call you at lunch tomorrow," Greg said, putting on his windbreaker. "I'm really curious as to how Carol Brightman and her attorney are going to react to your rejection of the countersuit."

"I'll call you if I hear from Joe," Tabby promised, walking him to the door.

"Be careful," Greg admonished as he kissed her good night.

He opened the door to leave. Tillie was standing there with a raised fist like she had just been about to knock when the door had been opened. She was crying.

15

"Tillie, what's the matter?" Tabby asked, motioning for her to enter the apartment.

"Cole is gone."

"What do you mean…gone?" Greg asked.

"We decided to postpone our honeymoon until October, so Cole returned to work. He worked the late shift tonight. He closed the store at eight and called me to see if I wanted wings from *Bailey's Bar and Grill* for supper. I said yes, and he said he would stop and get them on his way home. He asked me to call in the order; which I did," she responded in between sobs.

"Why do you think something has happened to him? Tabby asked the distraught woman.

"I gave him extra time to get home because he walks to and from work. I thought maybe he ran into someone at the bar from work and stayed to have a beer with them. An hour passed, and he still hadn't come home."

"Did you call the bar?" Greg asked.

"I did. They said that he never showed up to pick up the food order. I called the hardware store and it went right to the answering machine. So, I walked by his work and the place was in total darkness. I rapped on the door and no one answered," she replied. "I even went around to the delivery entrance in the back, but it was locked up tight."

"I'll call the sheriff," Greg said, stepping outside to make the call.

"I walked up and down both sides of Main Street thinking that maybe he fell and hurt himself, but he was no where to be found," Tillie said.

You sit down on the couch and I will make you a cup of tea while we wait for the sheriff to get here," Tabby suggested.

Tillie walked over to the front window and stood there looking out over Main Street. Tabby was amazed that in the short time that she had been married how much more confident and brave Tillie had become. The old Tillie would never walk around town in the dark. She would have hidden in her house and not done anything.

Greg returned from the outside deck and announced that the sheriff would be there shortly. Tabby thought that this would be a good time to ask Tillie about the photographer. It would take her mind of her missing husband.

"Here's your tea, Tillie. Come sit down," Tabby coaxed. "I need to ask you something."

"Is it something to help Cole?"

"It might be. Do you remember the photographer at your wedding? His name was Trevor Upton," Tabby started, watching Tillie's reaction. "You kept staring at him all day."

"Did I really? I hope that Cole didn't notice," she answered.

"Why were you staring at him? Did you recognize him from somewhere?" Tabby asked.

"I thought I did at first. He looked like someone I used to know from summer camp when I was younger."

"But, you don't think it was him now," Greg asked.

"We all change as we grow up. He looked like him, but the name was different. I made a mistake, I guess," she said, shrugging her shoulders.

"The boy at camp…do you remember his name?"

"Sure, I do. I had a mad crush on him. His name was Georgie Baker," Tillie answered.

"Where did you go to camp, Tillie?" Tabby inquired.

"At Camp Tomahawk in Carson's Bend. My brother and I went there every summer for ten years," she answered. "My sister never went because she didn't like bugs."

"You have been really helpful," Tabby said, patting her hand. "Drink your tea and try to relax. The sheriff should be here any minute."

Tabby walked to the kitchen with Greg right behind her.

"What's up? I saw that look on your face when she mentioned the kid's name."

"Shh... I'll tell you later. Tomorrow morning, I have to go back to Becky's Bakery and verify something before I know if I am right or not," Tabby replied.

A knock sounded on the door and Tabby yelled for the sheriff to come in. They all sat in the living room together and Tillie repeated her story. The sheriff was going to take Tillie home and put out an APB on Cole Brightman. He assured her that he and his deputies would be looking for him while they did their rounds during the night. Tillie left with the sheriff.

"So much for an early night," Greg said, getting ready to leave for a second time. "What about this Baker kid?"

"Cole's first wife's maiden name was Baker. It may just be a coincidence and it may not. I have to check it out in the morning before I go to the sheriff with my suspicions."

"Don't go anywhere else but the bakery unless you come get me," he insisted, kissing her goodnight again. "I mean it."

"I promise," she agreed as she closed the door and locked it.

The next day was another gorgeous beach day. The shop was slow, slow enough that Tabby decided to make a quick run to *Becky's Bakery* to check out her theory. She promised Janice that she would bring back some pastries for her to snack on.

Main Street was almost deserted. The heat drove people to the beaches at Fullers Point. The quietness of the beach days almost made up for the madness of the rainy days when people had nothing to do but shop and were cranky because they couldn't go to the beach.

Tabby reached the bakery and peeked in the window. Even though it was a beach day, people still had to eat. There was a fairly long line waiting at the counter. Tabby decided that this would be a good time to go in as she would have time to peruse the pictures on the wall while waiting in line.

She took her place in line. Becky didn't spot her at first as she was busy waiting on other customers. Tabby edged closer to the picture wall while keeping her place in line. Becky finally saw her and was watching Tabby's every move. She was not happy that her enemy was staring at the pictures on the wall.

Tabby smiled when she saw that she was right. Becky saw the smile and a look of terror crossed her face. The baker said something to her employee and disappeared out the back. Tabby bought a dozen mixed pastries and headed back to her shop.

This time, Tabby had the chance to test Becky's baking abilities. Her and Janice sampled the different pastries and agreed that they were good, really good. Becky did know what she was doing in the kitchen. While they ate, Tabby called Greg to tell him what she had found in the pictures, but he was out making a delivery.

She left him a message asking him to go into the bakery to look at the picture of the kids photographed at Camp Tomahawk and see if anyone looked familiar to him. She finished her message saying that she would talk to him at noon.

Sheriff Puckett came in early for his coffee. Tabby stepped into the back room and told him her suspicions. He said that he would check out her story and get back to her. He also informed her that they had not found any sign of Cole yet and he was still missing. But, at least now he had a viable direction to go in to find the missing man; Georgi Baker, AKA, Trevor Upton. He left with a full mug of coffee and two pastries.

Greg called at lunch time and said he received her message and did what she had asked him to do. He told her that he had gone into the bakery to look at the photos, but someone had taken them all down. When he asked where the photos were, one of the clerks told him that Becky was starting to pack up her personal things as a full asking price offer had been made to buy the bakery, equipment and all.

He said that he wouldn't see her for supper as he had some personal things to take care of having to do with his grandmother's Victorian house in Larsen. He said that he would call her when he got back in the morning. She asked if he sold the house, but he didn't answer. He had already hung up.

Business picked up towards the end of the day. Janice and Tabby were kept busy right until they locked the doors at five.

"Are you going to bingo tonight?" Tabby asked Janice as she closed out the register.

"Yes, Eric is calling. I don't like to play when he calls because I'm afraid that people will say he rigged it if I won. Once a month I volunteer at the concession stand so that is no accusations that Eric is dishonest. You know how those old people get when it comes to their bingo," Janice said, laughing.

"Tell me about it. Last time I went I sat in someone's seat that was a regular player. You'd think that I committed murder by sitting there. The only way that she would shut up was if I moved out of HER seat," Tabby said, rolling her eyes. "I haven't been back there since."

"They can get testy," Janice agreed. "What are you doing with Greg gone tonight?"

"I think that I am going to go out to the Whipper Will Drive-In after work to talk to Peter Walters about using the snack bar for the haunted house again this year; it's never too early to start planning these things," Tabby stated. "Peter finally won the lawsuit and regained ownership of the property. He's working on the buildings to bring them up to code so that he can open next summer. I want to talk to him before he leaves for Florida again."

"Be careful," Janice warned.

"I will. If Peter's not out there, I will come back home and cook a couple of batches of Blue Cinn jelly. We are running low on our summer special. And, I need to send an email to the local paper to put an ad in for the job opening that we now have," Tabby commented. "I wish my mother would call with Thelma's arrangements. We are going to have to close the store so that we can both go to the service."

"She'll call when all the arrangements have been made. I'll see you in the morning. I'll be here at eight," Janice said, leaving by the back door.

"Another day that I don't have to make a trip to the night deposit box, Tabby said, thinking out loud.

Ghost and Marmalade were waiting at the top of the stairs as usual. She fed them and changed into jeans and a sweatshirt to go to the drive-in.

"I'm going to your old stomping grounds," she said to the cats on her way out.

Tabby drove to the entrance of *The Whipper Will Drive-In.* A large sign had been placed at the end of the road announcing that the drive-in would reopen next year under new management. Tabby was so glad that she had played a part in stopping Larry Fink from selling the property to a condo developer. She spent many summer nights watching movies here and wanted her kids to do the same.

She drove up to the office, but it looked like everyone had left for the day. She wrote a quick note to Peter saying that had stopped by to talk to him and slipped it under the office door.

I guess it's home to do some cooking.

She drove down the dirt road that led back out to the north end of Main Street. She hadn't quite reached the end when she saw a white vehicle go by with Trevor Upton behind the wheel. She stepped on the gas to get to the end of the road so that she could see which direction he was taking; Route 132 to Carson's Bend or 127 to Larsen. He took the right at the split to Carson's Bend.

Several cars had passed in between her and Trevor's car. She decided to follow him; staying back far enough that he wouldn't see her, but close enough that she could still see if he turned off anywhere. She put her cell phone on silent and tucked it in her bra so that it couldn't be readily seen if something happened.

They traveled for almost twenty minutes before the white vehicle made a right off the main road. Tabby pulled over and waited a minute before she turned on to the road to leave a little distance between them. She drove slowly, skirting the large holes, while keeping an eye out for the white vehicle.

There were very few buildings in this stretch of the woods. Tabby spotted Trevor's white car in the driveway of a small cottage on the right side of the road. She continued past, hoping that he hadn't seen her drive by out of one of the windows in the house.

An abandoned cottage, five hundred feet up on the left, with a long driveway that swung around to the back of the house was just what Tabby needed to hide her vehicle. She had learned her lesson the hard way the last time she chased Larry Fink and didn't tell anyone where she was. A concussion and short hospital stay was something that she didn't want to repeat.

She pulled out her phone and called Greg. He didn't answer. She figured he must have been in whatever meeting it was that he needed to go to and turned off his phone. She left a message describing where she was and who she was following and then she tucked the cell phone away in her bra again.

Tabby sat there for a while watching the house. It was dusk, and it wouldn't be long before the woods around her would be pitch black. The headlights on Trevor's car came on and he left via the same way that he came in. Tabby opened the glove box and grabbed her flashlight. She waited a bit before she advanced towards the house making sure that Trevor was not going to return.

Turning on her flashlight, she shielded the light with her hand so that only small beams of light were coming through between her fingers and lighting up the road. She didn't want to twist an ankle in a hole as she walked. The cottage was in darkness.

She crept closer and looked in the first window that she came to. She couldn't see anything. Should she take a chance and shine the beam through the window to see what or who was inside? Before she could make the decision, she heard a stick snap behind her and she blacked out from a blow to the side of her head.

16

A short while later, Tabby regained consciousness. The room was lit with a battery powered lantern that was sitting on the table next to where Tabby lay on the floor tied up. She gave her eyes time to focus and then looked around the room to see who was there.

The cottage consisted of one large living space and several closed doors off to the back which Tabby assumed were bedrooms. In the far corner of the room she could see Cole Brightman, tied up and not moving. She didn't know if he was dead or alive.

She could hear a man and a woman talking in the kitchen area behind her.

"Now what are we going to do? Killing her wasn't part of the plan," the man said.

"It really doesn't matter. She stuck her nose in where it didn't belong and now she has to pay for it," the woman argued. "If Cole hadn't been such a social butterfly at the stupid wedding and sat down at the table like he was supposed to, both him and his rotten brother would be dead, and we would have been long gone by now."

"I knew it," Tabby said loudly. "You're Stephanie Baker, not Carol Brightman."

"Well look who decided to join the party," the woman said, walking towards Tabby from the kitchen area. "And yes, I am Stephanie Baker."

"And you're Georgie Baker, not Trevor Upton," Tabby stated, trying to sit up.

"It's George. I hated that name Georgie. That stupid Tillie Twittle gave me that name at camp and it stuck," he groused. "I never thought that she would recognize me after all these years. She hasn't changed at all; she's still a geek."

"She did recognize you, but she brushed it off because of the name change," Tabby stated. "Is Cole alive?"

"He is for now, but not for long. The small amounts of antifreeze that I have been feeding him is killing him in a nice, slow death," she said, smiling.

"Why? Why did you have to kill the Brightman brothers?" Tabby asked, now from a sitting position.

Before Stephanie could answer, a young boy, maybe three or four years old, came out of one of the bedrooms. He was holding a stuffed dragon and rubbing his eyes.

"I want a drink of water," he said.

"George, get the kid a cup of water and get him back in the bedroom," Stephanie ordered.

"You have a child?" Tabby asked.

"He's not my kid. He's Becky's brat," she answered as George led the boy back into the bedroom.

"Becky Tillman? He's her son? Does she know he's here?"

"Of course she doesn't. How do you think we get her to do what we want her to do? I've had to put up with that kid for way too long now," she complained. "Cousin's kid or not, it's time for him to go, too."

"You never answered my question. Why do you want the Brightman brothers dead? You left Cole; so why are you doing this to him?"

"Let's get your facts straight. I was married to Cole and very happy. I went out with my sisters one night to a bar and when I came out to go home, Jerry was hiding in the backseat of my car. He made me drive out to the dessert. He kept me captive in a small house for many months."

"You had no way to escape or get in touch with Cole?" Tabby asked.

"Jerry kept me locked in a cellar, chained to a wall by one ankle. He thought he could break me," she replied. "But, I never gave in to his wishes.'

"And just what were his wishes?"

"He wanted me to divorce Cole and marry him. After fourteen months of refusing to do it, he took me out in the dessert and beat me so severely that he figured I would die. He left me there for the scorpions and snakes to finish off."

"That was Jerry. But, what did Cole do to deserve this?"

"He never came to look for me and left me in the hands of his crazy brother."

"Now, girlfriend, you need to get your facts straight. Cole looked for you for three years. Jerry was the one that told Cole that you left him and that he had to move on. Jerry even tried to make him file for divorce, but Cole never would," Tabby said, stalling for time so that Greg could get her message and send help.

"Cole looked for me for three years? You're lying," she hissed.

George Baker had returned to the room to hear the end of the conversation. He shook his head while looking at his sister.

"Cole tried to find you?" he said. "See, if you had just made an effort to talk to him we wouldn't be in the position that we are in now. But, no, you had to stay mad and get revenge. You just had to believe all the lies that Jerry told you while you sat in that cellar."

"Shut up, you idiot. Can't you see that she is just trying to save their skins?" his sister yelled. "She'll get a double dose of antifreeze right before we leave and the two of them will die out here alone, just like I was left alone to die in the dessert."

"How did you figure out who we were?" George asked.

"When Tillie told me who she thought that you were, I remembered seeing a picture of a group of kids taken under a Camp Tomahawk sign on the bakery wall. I went back to check it and I recognized you and your sister in the picture. I recognized Carol as being Stephanie and the rest fell into place. Two things I haven't figured out yet; who is your attorney, Clifton Smith and how did Becky get involved in your little scheme?"

"You're going to die anyway, so what the heck," Stephanie commented.

"Clifton, or should I say Carl, is my real husband from California. He used to be an attorney, but he got disbarred for doing something illegal before we met. He does know his law though, and we have made mucho dinero off our scams. Geez, I must have been married at least twenty or so times in the last ten years and collected quite a bit of money as a widow that no one knew about. Mostly everyone is happy to settle out of court, until you came along and wouldn't."

"What about Becky? She is related to you?" Tabby asked, still stalling.

"Becky is our second cousin. She didn't even know that we existed until we broke into her trailer one night and took her kid. We sent her here to check to see if it was my Cole that was living here and told her to do what we told her to do or she'd never see her kid again," Stephanie bragged. "We've taken her kid twice and used her to help us. She knows if she does what we ask, she gets her brat back."

"She runs and hides, but Stephanie always seems to be able to find her," George added. "I tried to bring Becky here to visit her son as much as I could. I always had to blindfold her so that she wouldn't know where we were going."

"We heard gossip around your quaint little town that you like to solve mysteries. So, we had Becky keep you busy worrying about your boyfriend, Greg, and then we saw the opportunity to score some money in a wrongful death suit. Originally, we just came to town to wipe out the brothers."

"You came to town to wipe out Cole and Jerry," George insisted. "Not we."

"But it was you that put the poison in the jelly at the reception hall, George. I have a picture of you hiding behind a curtain so that you wouldn't be seen," Tabby stated.

"Oh. no! I'm not taking the rap for that. I was behind the curtain because I was checking some lens filters that took pictures in the dark. It is my dear sister that waltzed right in the back door delivering Becky's food to the caterer that put the poison in the jelly, not me," George protested.

"Nice, George, you're still a wimp; you'll never change," his sister claimed.

"You know what, Stephanie? I had a nice business building up in California until you blackmailed me to come here to get you into the reception hall. You didn't need me, you had Becky."

"George, you're right. I didn't need you and if I hadn't brought you along, this whole thing might not have blown up like it has because you were recognized," Stephanie said, pulling a gun out of her sweatshirt pocket. "I guess that I don't need you anymore, either."

"Seriously? I'm your brother," George answered, the fear evident in his eyes.

"And your point is?" Stephanie said, pointing the gun at her brother. "All right, I guess I need you around for a while longer. We didn't get the money from Miss Nosy over there, so I guess we have to hide out here just a little while longer until the bakery sells and then I will trade Becky the money from the sale for her son's life. It wouldn't be the first time that she sold her bakery to get her son back."

"George, make a run to the *Outdoor Café* and pick us up a couple of burgers," Stephanie ordered. "All this talking is making me hungry."

"Don't kill anyone until I get back," George insisted, picking up his car keys.

"Yea, yea, just go get the food, "she answered, waving the gun back and forth.

George left, and Tabby continued to stall her captor.

"So, if you've been staying here, where is your husband?" Tabby asked.

"Carl returned to California to take care of paperwork for another scam that we are running on the West coast," she replied, matter-of-factly.

Cole groaned and moved around in the corner. He didn't look good, and Tabby knew that she had to get him help and quick. Stephanie heard the groan, too.

"Don't worry, Cole. I'll be right there with more juice for you," Stephanie said, walking to the kitchen area.

She left the gun on the kitchen counter and walked by Tabby holding a glass full of juice and antifreeze.

"Oh. no, you don't," Tabby yelled, tripping her as she went by.

The glass flew out of Stephanie's hand and she hit the floor, hard. The front door crashed open and Sheriff Puckett and Deputy White were on top of Stephanie before she could get up.

They had apprehended George as he was climbing into his car. Watching through the window, they were just waiting for the moment that Stephanie would lay down the gun so that they could enter without anyone getting shot. They cuffed the screaming woman and she bit Deputy White as he forced her into his cruiser. Sheriff Puckett untied Tabby and helped her up onto the couch.

"Cole is in bad shape. She's been feeding him small doses of antifreeze," Tabby stated.

"George told us. We've already called for an ambulance," Sheriff Puckett confirmed. "Are you okay?"

"I'm good. I think that my head is getting used to this. I don't even have a headache this time."

"Not funny, Miss Moon," the sheriff said, frowning. "Not funny at all."

Greg was allowed in after they had Stephanie cuffed and out of the house. He sat down next to Tabby on the couch and held her hand.

"At least you called me this time," he said, half-smiling.

"I did try," she insisted. "Don't messages count for anything?"

"I'll let you know after I have you home safely," Greg answered.

"Oh, geez! Sheriff Puckett, come with me," Tabby said, springing up from the couch.

The sheriff and Greg followed her to the far back bedroom. She opened the door and flipped on the light. Hiding under the bed, terrified by all the noise coming from the living room, was Becky's son. Tabby laid on the floor to talk to him.

"What's your name?" she asked, quietly.

"Trevor," he answered.

"Is your name Trevor Upton?"

"Yup."

"I think your mommy has been waiting to see you," Tabby said.

"Can I go see my mommy now? I've been good, I really have," he whispered.

"If you come out from under the bed, my friends and I will bring you to see your mommy. Do you want to go for a ride in a police car?"

"Okay," he agreed, crawling out from under the bed. "I'm hungry."

"I bet that your mommy will make you something special to eat, Tabby said, picking up the young boy. She turned to Greg and the sheriff.

"I'd like you to meet the real Trevor Upton, Becky Tillman's son," she announced. "The Baker's have been holding him hostage to keep control over Becky and making sure that she did what they demanded of her. Greg, remember when Joe said that Becky put on a mask when they drove away in the car. She had bought a dinner for her and her son and had to agree to be blindfolded so that she wouldn't know where they were keeping him."

"So, they kept her son from her so that she would help them?" Sheriff Puckett asked.

"Yes, and it wasn't the first time that they had kidnapped him," Tabby answered. "I'll explain everything later. Now, let's get Trevor back with his mommy."

Tabby rode in the back of the cruiser with the young boy, while Greg drove her car back to his house. The sheriff put on the lights and the siren as they rode to the utter delight of their young passenger. When they hit town, the sheriff shut off the siren, but left the lights going. They pulled up to the front of Becky's house.

Sheriff Puckett opened the back door to the cruiser as Becky opened her front door. Tabby crawled out with Trevor. He spotted his mommy and took off running. Becky ran towards him, scoping her son up in her arms and burying her face in his neck while she cried. Greg had pulled into his driveway, next door and was watching through the car window.

Becky walked up to Tabby and the sheriff.

"I knew that you would help me," she said to Tabby through her tears.

"It was you who stuck the note on my back door?" Tabby asked, as Greg walked up and joined the group.

"I was too afraid to sign it. I didn't want them to hurt my son," she answered.

"I'm hungry," Trevor said again.

"It's getting late and the lights are drawing a crowd," Sheriff Puckett commented. "You go in and feed that boy of yours and I will be over in the morning to take your statement.

"Stephanie and George?"

"They won't bother you ever again. They are going away for a very long time," the sheriff answered.

Becky smiled and thanked them.

"I'm going in and feed my little man," she announced, hugging her son.

"Mommy, you quishin' me," Trevor complained.

"Yes, I am," she said, turning and walking to her house.

She waved as she closed the door.

"I wonder if she'll stay now," Tabby commented.

"Time will tell. Do you want to go to the hospital and get your head checked out?" the sheriff asked Tabby.

"No. I just want to go home, take a shower and crawl into bed," Tabby answered.

"I'll be in your shop in the morning to take your statement as well," Sheriff Puckett stated. "Greg, it seems like it's turning into a full-time job watching over this one."

"Yes, sir, it is. But, it's a job that I will willingly accept," Greg said, smiling at his fiancé.

"Better you than me. I gave up years ago," the sheriff sighed. "I'll see you in the morning; have the coffee on."

Tabby and Greg walked back to her car.

"You want me to come stay with you?" Greg asked, putting his arm around her waist.

"No, I'll be fine, really."

"I think I finally understand why you do what you do," he said. "I saw

Becky's face when she saw her son. I am so proud of what you accomplished tonight even though I was terrified for your safety."

"It was pretty cool, wasn't it?" Tabby asked, snuggling her head down into Greg's shoulder. "I hope that I didn't disturb your meeting tonight."

"No, it was pretty much over before it began," he answered.

"I'm sorry."

"It's okay. Something else will come up," he replied. "You better get going. We both have to get up early tomorrow,"

"Yea, you're right. Tomorrow night…a nice quiet supper at my place?" she whispered.

"Ill be there," he promised, giving her a long goodnight kiss and opening her car door for her to leave.

17

Over the next week, Tabby received many visits from the sheriff. The FBI even showed up at her shop as they had been brought in on the Baker case because their scams crossed state lines.

Tabby was glad that Becky decided to keep her bakery and become a permanent resident of the town. Once Gladys circulated her version of Becky's sad tale, the town rallied behind her and forgave her for her terrible behavior and all the trouble that she had caused. Her bakery flourished, and she made many new friends.

Cole was on his way to a full recovery.

The day before the Fourth, Tabby received the second of her reward checks. This one was for fifteen thousand from the insurance company that insured the bank. She now had the ten-thousand-dollar deposit that was required to make a bid on the Piper house at the sealed envelope auction. She would tell Greg the next day at the town picnic.

Fourth of July rolled in with a bang, literally. Someone threw a firecracker up in the air near Tabby's front window where the cats were laying in the morning sun beam. It exploded, sending the cats flying into Tabby's bedroom and up inside her box spring. She tried for ten minutes to get them to come out, but they stayed steadfast in their hiding place.

She returned to the kitchen to finish packing the picnic basket that Greg, her mother, and herself would share at the outing on the town green after the parade. Greg picked her up at nine-thirty and they walked up to the green to sit and watch the parade as it proceeded down Main Street. Tabby's mother joined them on the blanket after the parade.

As they ate, people came and went, sitting with them to visit. Jen and Bea brought a picnic basket with them. They joined Tabby and company, combining the food they bought with what Tabby had brought, forming one large smorgasbord. Richard Wells, the town elder, stopped by to say hello.

When it was just the close-knit group and no visitors, Tabby asked for quiet.

"I have an announcement to make," she started. "I have finally received my reward money for recovering the stolen bank money. I have a very special use in mind for it. Can anyone guess what it might be?"

"A new car?" Jen suggested.

"No. Anyone else?"

There was no more guessing.

"I am using it for the deposit to be able to put a bid in on the Piper house. When Greg and I get married, that is where we would like to live," she announced.

Greg and Samantha looked at each other.

"So, when are you getting married?" Bea asked.

"I still don't know. Well, I do know, but I haven't talked to Greg about it yet," Tabby answered.

"You know? Greg asked.

"Yes, I do."

"Well, when are you going to tell the rest of us?" her mother asked.

"Yea, when are you going to tell the rest of us?" Greg repeated, smiling broadly.

"I guess that I could tell you right now, if it's okay with Greg," Tabby replied.

"Yes! I am finally getting a definite date," he said, high-fiving Samantha.

"I decided on Halloween night, next year," Tabby announced. "On our first date, Greg said that he was sure that someday I would have the fancy Halloween wedding that I missed out on with Finn. So, I am now going to have that Halloween wedding with Greg."

"I, for one, wouldn't have expected anything different from my daughter. Congratulations to both of you," Samantha said, reaching over to hug them both.

"And I want Jen to be my Maid of Honor," Tabby requested of her best friend.

"Greg, don't you have something to tell Tabby?" Samantha inquired.

"You will have to find another use for that money," Greg said, frowning.

"What do you mean?"

"I told you a made-up date for the auction. I wanted to buy the house and surprise you with it as a wedding gift. The night that I went to Larsen, I went to the auction. But, I lost out to another bidder. I lost the house to Samuel Benson," Greg stated. "He bid really high because he wanted the house that his mom loved so much."

"That's okay. Samuel does love that house as much as we do, maybe even more," Tabby replied. "We have over a year to find another house before we get married."

"I have an announcement to make, too," Samantha claimed. "I know that everyone has been asking about Thelma's service. It seems she updated her will and doesn't want anything but a small private service with just the people she listed to be in attendance. And… she wants her ashes spread out over Fullers Point on Christmas Day while the invited guests sing Jingle Bell Rock."

"Way to go, Thelma!" Greg exclaimed. "She's going to go out in song!"

"She's already been cremated and is sitting in an urn in my room at the bed and breakfast. Her daughter will return for the reading of the will next month before school starts," Samantha stated. "The official announcement will be in the paper next week."

"On that note, anyone want to go to *The Local Scoop* and get a triple decker ice cream cone?" Greg asked.

"Seriously? You haven't eaten enough already?" Tabby laughed.

"There is always room for ice cream. Right, my soon to be mother-in-law?"

"Whatever my soon to be son says," Samantha agreed.

"Am I going to be out-voted the rest of my life by you two?" Tabby laughed.

"The rest of your life, Miss Tabitha Flower Moon; the rest of your life," Greg said, as he leaned over to seal the deal with a kiss.

THE END

RECIPE

Backwoods Al's Berrie Company Peach Jam

- 2 pounds of peaches (fresh or frozen)
- 5 ½ cups of sugar
- 1 package of pectin
- 1 teaspoon lemon juice
- 2 large pans and covers
- Wooden spoon and ladle
- 8 jelly jars and covers

Place 8 jelly jars and their covers into boiling water in a separate pan. Make sure they are submerged completely in the water. Let boil.

Pit and shred peaches by hand and place in a large sauce pan with lemon juice and bring to a boil. Slowly stir in pectin and bring back to a boil.

Add sugar, continuously stirring the mixture until all sugar is dissolved. Once dissolved, let the mixture come to a rolling boil for one minute.

Wearing heat resistance gloves, fill each jar using the ladle as it is removed from the boiling water, screw on the cover and turn upside down for one minute to seal the jar.

Yield: 7 to 8, 8oz jars

Variation… add cinnamon to taste to make a Peach Cobbler Jelly.

Printed in the USA
CPSIA information can be obtained
at www.ICGtesting.com
LVHW020237211124
797240LV00025B/322